CW01481214

Dressing Up

Short Stories

Daphne Glazer

*To Margaret
with lots of love

from Daphne.*

IRON
PRESS

First Published 1994 by Iron Press
5, Marden Terrace, Cullercoats,
North Shields, Northumberland NE30 4PD, UK
Tel: (091) 253 1901

Typeset by David Stephenson
in New Century Schoolbook 10 point

Printed by Peterson Printers
South Shields

ISBN 0 906228 51 4

Acknowledgements: *A Wonder of the World, The Butterfly*
and *Out of the Question* were first broadcast on BBC Radio 4.
Stage Struck was first published in IRON magazine.
The remaining stories are previously unpublished.

IRON Press books are represented by:
Password Books Ltd
23 New Mount Street
Manchester M4 4DE
Tel: (061) 953 4009
Fax: (061) 953 4001

Yorkshire & Humberside
ARTS

for Peter, Imo and Sebastian as ever.

DAPHNE GLAZER, a Sheffielder, who worked for five years in Lagos, Nigeria, teaching German for the Goethe-Institut, now lives in Hull with her family and parrot, Squawter. She has made toffees and also taught in various institutions including a maximum security prison and a Borstal. Currently she is a lecturer at Hull College.

Her stories are broadcast regularly on Radio 4 and have appeared in such publications as *New Statesman and Society*, *The Guardian*, *Critical Quarterly*, *Panurge*, *IRON*, and have been included in anthologies. Her novel THREE WOMEN was published in 1984 by Piatkus Press, and her first collection of short stories, THE LAST OASIS in 1992 by the Sumach Press.

The Stories

Dressing Up

When Kim announced to Mam that she'd got a job in 'Cherry Ripe', the naughty knickers' shop, it was as though a bomb exploded.

"You haven't..."

"Yes, I have... well, what's wrong with that anyway?"

"It's discustin'... don't know what your Dad'll say."

Mam worked in an insurance office and wore crisp white blouses and full skirts in summer that bunched at the waist and dingled about mid-calf. In winter it was straight navy skirts and always safe navy court shoes and she toted her square navy handbag.

Dad painted and decorated for a living, but never liked giving their house the treatment, however Mam insisted, and every year there'd be new flower-squiggled wall-paper springing out all over. Kim felt it was all so boring, so tame... She was sick of being bored.

On her way to school for years and years she'd been staring at 'Cherry Ripe'. It had a green and red striped awning above the windows to shield them from the sun and she'd often see a woman poling away, letting the awning down on bright days.

When the bus ground to a halt close by it, all heads would turn, particularly male ones and Kim had thought that the bus might even topple over, zapped down by 'Cherry Ripe' magnetism.

All the lads on the school bus hooted and peered and the girls wanted to look but restrained themselves because of the lads.

During the time when she'd been at school, supposedly wrestling with 'Deutsch Heute', algebra and other sleep-inducing subjects, the thought of the shop had set her imagination skipping: what would you see if you went in? What if people spotted you entering? The woman poling the canopy up and down looked normal, maybe even a bit fuddy, rather like Mam. That made it more intriguing than ever. Perhaps they used the canopy to prevent people looking in... and it wasn't as though you dared linger outside.

A million folk stories had grown up around 'Cherry Ripe': they sold all manner of exotic lingerie - sexy, dubious things that you might see women wearing in the men's mags that Mr Towser, the newsagent, a medallion man, kept on his top shelf - titles like 'Men Only' and 'Mayfair'. There might be other contraptions too, stuff you wouldn't have heard of... all exciting and forbidden, hinting at perversions.

All men, Mam had always made clear, were dangerous rapists and monsters underneath. You had to watch out. Other lasses always said: They're only after one thing.

Basically school had not been for her - she'd taken to twagging in the last year and wandering round the shops with her mate, trying on tops and leggings in 'Miss Selfridge' and spraying herself with the perfume testers in 'Boots' and having the odd fag.

Then had come the 'schemes' and they'd been deadly - one in a greengrocer's where you got earth in your nails and had to lug boxes about; the other in a laundry that made you sweat and use tons of deodorant. So when she saw the ad. in the evening paper for a sales assistant at 'Cherry Ripe' - 'Must be personable' - she'd rung up straight away and been given an appointment, though she didn't know what 'personable' meant. This real sensible older woman had interviewed her.

"Well, dear, you see we get all sorts coming in here, the customers that is - you have to be able to deal with..." Her voice had trailed off, leaving Kim to speculate. "You look all right though... I'm sure Mr King will think so."

What did she mean? Kim was twiggy and had helped-on blonde hair and was given to wearing black leggings and black tops and looked about twelve, which annoyed her.

"Mr King's the boss, the owner, but we don't get to see him much - he has a gallery."

"Oh..." (What did you do in a gallery?)

"Anyway, you'll be all right - I'll be here at first mostly. I'll show you how to carry on."

Now, faced with Mam's forebodings and fury, Kim tried to look glum. Inside she was chortling and still running through the pictures of 'Cherry Ripe's' interior. Straight facing you as you went in, and balanced above the glass-fronted drawers, which contained bras and knickers and other exciting things, were thigh-high black leather boots with six inch stiletto heels - heels as thin and slick as daggers. She couldn't take her eyes off them and imagined herself prancing about in a pair on stage and singing whilst a group of black-haired, stunningly handsome men in evening dress closed in behind her and then swung her up in the air. It would be great to be another 'Madonna', only different.

A message on the counter caught her eye. It said:

'Your fantasies begin here.'

Everywhere were show-cards of women wearing lacy bras who beamed shyly out at the customers or looked sweetly serious. Then near the boots she'd noticed a poster of two blonde girls with smoky eyes, rather like herself, kissing and doing things to each other - what she couldn't tell. They were both wearing black dresses and not much underneath except for some g-string type efforts. Pushed to one side was another display card of two blondes but this was really a picture of girls' bums. Their knickers had got sucked into the crack between the globes. Just looking at that had made her feel uncomfortable, because it reminded her of being at school, and when your knickers were wearing out, they'd creep up and lodge in your crotch and chafe. It seemed daft wearing such a thing, it was bound to rub you.

Whilst she was still pondering about that, Mam was letting fly.

"You don't know... I bet there's some right oddments go in that shop... and I mean to say..."

"Mam it's just like Marks & Spencer's really." That wasn't strictly true but still. If M & S didn't line all the underwear up on racks and if they'd had a few display cards, it might have looked nearer 'Cherry Ripe'.

"It's not for young girls," Mam kept at it, "it leads men on..."

Kim noticed that Mam's cheeks had turned pink. She felt a faint ripple pass over her, something that moved between fear and pleasure - 'leads men on'... bloody hell! She pictured the buses swaying, all tilting at an angle as men cricked their necks trying to gaze into the windows.

"Well it's better than nowt." That was the trump card. Work was a very important word in their family. She often heard Dad rumbling on about 'scroungers' and 'If kids want to work, they'll find it. There's no such thing as can't get a job'.

Mam didn't like it but she was having to accept that for the time being Kim was forced to work in a house of ill repute.

"You'll have to try to get out of there as quick as you can, Kim - I daren't tell your Dad where you're workin' - he'd have a fit."

So she was now going to penetrate the mysteries for herself. She'd always loved lacy pants and bras and here were drawers packed with cellophane bags each containing a folded bra.

As she approached the shop on her first morning, she kept peering about her, trying to be sure that no men were watching. Her cheeks blazed. She caught a brief glimpse of corselets, bustiers, teddies - all in white, scarlet, mauve and black - displayed in the window. A bald model was strapped into a black and white corselet, which sported two hearts over the crotch and fastened in front with hooks. A lacy suspender belt and blue and white frilly garters held up the white stockings.

"Hello, love, come in!" Suzy, the chief assistant, mummied her. She was wearing a white blouse, black skirt and hairy black cardigan and didn't seem to fit in with the shop at all: Mam in her insurance office gear. "Your name's Kim, isn't it?"

Kim nodded and smiled, her eyes zipping all over the place.

On the counter she caught sight of another notice.

'Don't be afraid to give your requirements, nothing surprises us.'

A shiver made the goosepimples rise on her back and forearms. What sort of surprises were in store, because a notice like that must mean something?

During that first day she learnt what was in the glass fronted drawers: lace-trimmed briefs and ivory-coloured silk bras with the thinnest of straps and matching silk pants; flowered french knickers in the palest blue, maroon and purple nestled in cellophane packets. They were made of slippery satin and had wide flappy legs that made you think of ladies in 1920s films - ladies in satin dressing-gowns and with their eyebrows plucked into thin black lines above their huge sleepy eyes. She couldn't stop examining the merchandise. It thrilled her. The white whalebone corsets with hook fastenings right up the front made her laugh.

"I wouldn't fancy one of them," she told Suzy.

"No, love, they'd be a bit warm I should think, particularly if you was carrying a bit of weight."

Black pvc cat suits, trousers, minis hung up on a discreet rail behind a display fixture.

"Oh, and we've got these, Kim," Suzy said, slapping down some rubberised objects on the counter - there was a top which looked like a skinny sleeveless T-shirt. Another package contained some pants.

"Bloody hell!" Kim said, "what do they want them for? Must be that hot, and it smells..."

"They say it's the feel," Suzy said, and wouldn't elaborate. Kim ran her fingers over them. Yes, they did feel smooth, as smooth as flesh or silk.

Obviously girls wouldn't be wearing such yucky stuff for their own pleasure - anyway they must look weird in them. But what kind of men would buy this gear?

The first customer turned out to be a woman after a black 32A bra which they didn't happen to have but Suzy searched through the drawers and tweaked open countless packets to display their contents on the glass counter top. It all seemed quite nice and cosy and the girls on the display cards looked on, giving coy smiles.

After that the postman barged in with a parcel which he banged down on the counter top as fast as he could. He took care to keep his eyes averted from the display cards and the models and was in and out in a blink as though fearing an attack.

At midday a well-dressed man in a suit came in and approached Kim who blushed. Suzy was having her nosh in the back.

"Oh, hello..." He had a very posh accent, she noticed, "I wonder if you've a red silk bra, 38C cup?"

Kim flurried in the drawers. There followed the ritual of getting out the boxes of envelopes, pulling out bras and displaying them on the glass. The man nodded and touched them with fine pale hands. No scarlet C cup - he could have black. He took the black and three pairs of french knickers (large) - all silk.

She folded them and slid them back into their packets. What would his girlfriend be like? Kim imagined a tall lass with great boobs and silky blond shoulder-length hair. Her scarlet nail varnish would be perfect and her diamonds as big as Disprins.

Just when she was slipping the lot into a green and scarlet striped bag Suzy re-emerged from the back premises.

"Oh, hello..." she smiled at the man and he grinned.

"Not very warm is it."

"No, mind you, what can we expect - nearly Christmas?"

His pin-stripe suit disappeared through the door.

"Somebody's getting a nice prezzie!" Kim said.

"Oh, that's for him."

"You don't mean it!"

"Oh yes, he's a reg'lar... one of our usuals - did I tell you, Mr King likes to know what we've sold and who to. There's a calendar in the back - best make a note of this one."

"Why does he like to know?"

"Couldn't say."

A succession of men followed but most of those seemed to be buying presents for girlfriends or lovers. They didn't look the sort who'd be getting stuff for their wives.

Just before closing time a big man with beer-coloured hair and nostrils like tunnels and bulgy brown eyes strode in. He was buttoned into a grey lounge suit. The shop vibrated with a deep spicy scent of after-shave. Kim noticed his heavy gold identity bracelet and his signet ring.

"Oh, Mr King, hello."

"Everything going okay, Suzy?"

His eyes shot over Kim in passing and Kim's back and arms sprouted goosepimples. He was a wolf, she was sure of it. She thought of Mam's words.

"Yes, fine Mr King - this is our new assistant, Kim."

"Ah yes."

He didn't seem interested and went off with Suzy into the back to discuss something. Kim supposed she must be giving him a run-down of the sales.

She continued to stare about her at the bustiers and packets of fish-net stockings on display. Beside her was a box of 'Dickie Bows' with the caption above them:

'Make sure your willy comes smart!'

Another box was labelled 'Chastity Belts for Men'.

After work Kim got home to find Mam frying the beefburgers and chips.

"How did it go, love?"

"Oh all right - Suzy, the other girl - well, she's a woman - shows you what to do."

"There wasn't...?"

Mam's thoughts were running on rapists and seducers, Kim could see, and it made her think of Mr King. "No, nothing like that," she said, "just like any other shop."

"Do take care."

Every morning Mam said, "Take care, mind how you go," and gave Kim a certain look. It was one that Dad couldn't interpret. She was also ready with the list of job vacancies in the evening paper when Kim got back.

Things had settled into a certain routine by this time. Kim was used to the mainly male customers - ones like the university lecturer with his frog-spawny eyes wriggling in the ripples of his lenses, who bought a waitress's outfit - a black apron with a frilly white edge and a little white cap; black fish-net stockings and a black lace suspender belt. He just looked a bit nervous and intense during the whole proceedings of selecting the items and packing them into a plain white plastic bag. Others would stand there clopping a ten p coin on the glass counter and whistling to themselves to cover their embarrassment.

On this particular day - a Friday, late on, just before Christmas - Suzy had whizzed off to do a bit of Christmas shopping, leaving Kim in charge. It was dark outside and she could see the neon legs and red stilettos winking on the sign in the window.

A group of fellers in their twenties were hanging about by the shop door, banging into one another and yelping with laughter. Kim felt a dither of fear. What were they getting up to? Then the door opened. The gust of beery breath smacked her nostrils.

"Hiya... now then, Miss... have you got any, er..." Here the one speaking was nudged by his mate.

"Go on... ask her then... ger it out."

They were red in the face with booze and excitement. Kim stared at them. They reminded her of lads at junior school.

"Yes?" she said.

"Have you gor any of them knickers with a hole in?"

Kim slid the crotchless brief box out. Privately she thought they were stupid. Your pubic hair pushed through the holes as though it had gone mad or turned into some little furry creature.

"Fer the girlfriend."

Then they wanted bras with nipple holes in.

"Your girlfriends'll not want these," she said, sounding, she thought, like Suzy, her voice quite flat. "Bet you'll be bringing this lot back after Christmas."

But they bumbled out on a wave of hilarity and beer, clutching their striped packages of crotchless briefs and nipple-exposing bras, apparently well pleased.

Kim watched them lurching their way round the corner.

Two men in suits appeared and they bought diaphanous nighties and silk briefs.

No sooner had they gone, than she saw the big form of Mr King. Her heart pattered. He'd only been in a couple of times since she'd started working there.

"Ah, hello," he said, "you on your own?"

"Yes, Mr King, I'm just about closing up."

"That's right - you might as well call it a day now." He let the yale snap down and turned the card to closed. Kim saw an early slice of moon floating in the black sky, the legs winked. She was feeling nervous but she didn't know why - Mr King spooked her, though he was also attractive in a weird way.

"How's it going, Kim?"

He had actually called her by her name and he sounded kind and even interested.

"Oh, fine, Mr King. Things are selling quite well."

"What things?"

She found she couldn't pronounce the word 'crotchless', so she rummaged in her mind for a euphemism. "Oh well, you know, the er..." The word crotchless expanded and expanded until it suggested rampant cucumbers and writhing pythons and she couldn't bring herself to say it.

"Yes?"

He was gazing at her, lifting an eyebrow. His aftershave threw an aura round him.

"The briefs with holes," she finished.

"Ah. What about pvc? Suzy tells me it's old hat now - the market's gone."

"No, we've not sold much of that - it'll be too sweaty I expect."

"Quite."

She was about to fetch her coat, when Mr King stopped her. Was he going to pounce on her, drag off her clothes and make violent, painful love to her? She thought he must hear the clanging of her heart. They were standing very close to each other, but she only came up to his middle jacket button. He was wearing a charcoal grey lounge suit with a white mac over it.

The world stopped as Kim waited.

"Would you like to do a spot of modelling for me, Kim?"

"My mother'll be cooking the tea."

"It won't take long."

"All right then."

"Find yourself a pair of boots and a corselet - make it red and black... whatever you like... just get dressed up and then come out. I'll be in the back."

It was fun getting into the massive boots, the red satin briefs and the black satin corselet - just like some stage performance - but at the same time she felt a bit daft. What was he going to do? What would she do if he tried anything on? One kick from the stilettos would disable a man, she decided.

When she tottered into the kitchen, he was sitting in an old armchair, warming his hands before the two-bar electric fire. A big black bag squatted beside him and a tripod had been set up.

"Just a few shots," he said.

There followed what seemed like ages of poses, with Kim lying on the sofa over which a silky cloth had been draped, and kicking her legs in the air; or Kim bending down with her backside facing the camera and her face peering round grinning; or Kim leaning forward so her front popped out of the corselet.

Nothing was ever right first time. She must repeat the poses endlessly whilst the big black snout of Mr King's camera probed and pressed. It became part of him, thrusting, waggling. By this time she was covered with goosepimples because the little electric fire only took the chill off the air and, to add to her misery, the briefs had sunk into the crack of her bum.

"Just another couple," he muttered.

It was whilst he was re-loading his camera that they heard blows being thundered on the shop door and someone bellowing.

"Who the hell's that? You'd best get dressed." Mr King instructed.

Before Kim had had chance to change back into her own clothes, Mr King had been forced to open the shop door, and she came face to face with her Dad.

"What for buggering hell's sake do you think you're doin'?" Dad's face was brick-red with fury. "And you," he'd turned on Mr King, who was also very red in the face, "you want lockin' up, you pervert! You'll have no daughter of mine workin' here. I could smash your face in! Get that muck off!" he snarled at Kim.

As Kim struggled out of the gear into her own clothes, she listened for the sounds of Mr King being flattened, but could only hear her Dad ranting on.

"You want closing down," were Dad's last words to Mr King, as he marched Kim out of 'Cherry Ripe'.

They got into Dad's van that ponged of paint fumes and he drove home, still fulminating.

"Your Mam was real worried... worried out of her mind. That's when she told me - look at t' time! Look at it!"

"But Dad, he didn't do anything."

"No, and by God, he'll not get the chance to, neither..."

Later when they were sitting in the kitchen eating shepherd's pie, carrots and mashed spuds, Kim tried to explain but they weren't going to listen.

"Mam, it's not what you think... it's like playing games... it's just looking... they don't *do* anything... nobody does things... it's just dressing up."

"It leads men on."

"It's perverted."

Mam and Dad got quite excited about the dark and dangerous perversions of 'Cherry Ripe'. In fact Kim hadn't seen them so animated for a long time. Why must they go on about SEX, hint, hint, as though it was some devilish number... it obviously wasn't if it needed tarting up so much... in fact it must be a downright yawn. It was really a relief that she wouldn't be working there any longer - but it wasn't because of anything other than a longing for some new games. 'Cherry Ripe' was okay, but it was no joke being stuck in the kitchen with old Kingy and being frozen for several hours when she wanted her tea. Anyway, it was all a bit daft.

Next time, she decided, she wanted something that gave her a chance to use her initiative - that was the buzz word in the job centres - initiative - and a bit of excitement. Maybe she'd have a nice dragon-fly tattooed on her midriff and join a circus, or do sky-diving...

The Butterfly

Glenda's wishing like mad that she hasn't taken up the dare. She can't imagine what came over her. At the time, things just seemed to get out of hand. It's the Saturday of Bob Scott's retirement party and they've all been having a buffet lunch which has extended into something more, because this daft game started: people daring one another to do things.

Dare you to go and have a tattoo done, Glend, Kev from Accounts challenged. People had been taking their trousers off; kissing those they'd always hated and the ones they'd secretly loved; warbling solos; and then it was her turn. She could have said no, but somehow that was impossible. Everybody else accepted their dares, even throwing a cream cake in the office manager's face and then licking the cream off, just as though they'd become other people, ones you didn't know. That was what made it exciting: people were familiar and yet strange, and they were doing the unexpected.

Glenda turns into this narrow street of red-brick terraces and drives slowly along, glancing to left and right for the tattooist that Kev described.

Why am I doing this? she asks herself. Have I gone crazy? What will Evan think? He's her live-in boyfriend and works in the Accounts Department of the Gas Offices. Evan wears white shirts and boring ties and a leather bomber jacket and well-cut dark-grey trousers. He doesn't like anything vulgar or loud and he prefers to see her in a nice little dress rather than leggings or a mini and a little top. They've been living together for three years. During the party, all of a sudden she'd felt drab in her flowered cotton dress and strappy sandals. The other girls were wearing leggings and baggy T-shirts blobbed with sunbursts and twirls, one or two had such short minis that the men were asking them to pick up pound coins and five pound notes from the floor.

There's the tattooist's. It leaps out at her from the continuous line of orange-brick houses. Lenny's Tattooing. Painted on the window is a beast wearing jeans. His head is a skull and he has vampire claws for hands and he is emerging from some choppy blue waves. Behind him is a raucous red and yellow sky. Messages are printed down the window supports. She wonders what they all mean. What a place to be visiting!

What if anyone sees her going in? Well, it's only a bet... but what about Evan? He'll never get over it.

As she climbs out of her Mini, she almost turns back. They don't believe she'll go through with it. She can see Kevin Hamilton laughing at her - a real clever clogs. He thinks she's too scared; that he's got her number. Normally he'll not joke with her like he does with Sammy and Natasha. They always have their computers decorated with furry bees and little stickers and cards and pot animals that someone's given them... and there's all that secret giggling. But not for her. She's the sensible type who gets on with the correspondence and stays behind to finish letters and nobody ever makes a pass at her... not that she would expect it of course... but then again, it is a little ego-boost to have the odd admirer.

As she's locking up her car, she's staring at the figure rising from the waves. It all looks really tacky and it makes her nervous. The street is hot and quiet. She sees a notice on the door - 'Open 11-5. Sunday by appointment' and then 'Gone to Clary' and an arrow pointing down the street.

Now she can turn round, get back in the car and drive away, but she doesn't. Instead she walks down the road in the direction of the little pub at the bottom.

She pushes open the door. The bar is crowded with men, all with pint glasses standing before them. How will she recognise the tattooist? But it's obvious... A man is staring at her. He has ice-blue eyes and his hair is shaved close to his skull and there's a scar down his cheek.

The reason she knows he must be the one, is because of his arms: from wrist to shoulder they are covered with intricate blue, green and red patterns. The designs are so dense and intricate that he seems to be wearing a long-sleeved shirt. She can't stop staring at them. There are snakes, dragons, flowers and scales that remind her of fishes. His arms are magic landscapes and have a life of their own. They're another presence. He is exotic, sitting there at the bar beside the chaps in suits. She's seen pictures in old Geographical Magazines at school of forgotten tribal people in the Amazon Basin, their naked bodies clothed in strange designs.

So intent has she been that she hasn't realised how she has been staring. Now he is gazing back at her. The icy blueness of his eyes doesn't change. He's sizing her up.

"Oh, er... hello," she mutters, "are you the, er, tattooist?"

"Yer," he says, and gives her this open indifferent stare.

She feels now that this is an important occasion but she doesn't know why.

"I, er..."

"Yer?"

She is drawn again to the patterns on his arms. They continue around his collar bones. The sleeveless white T-shirt prevents her seeing the full extent of their decorations. He has a thick gold hoop in one ear.

"Do you do roses or butterflies?"

"Yer."

She notices that his teeth are little and stained with nicotine. A thin ginger moustache feathers his upper lip.

"Would you, er, be able...?"

"Sure... when?"

"Er, now."

"Look," he says, and his tone is brutal, so that she finds herself blushing, "if you're not sure, don't."

Her skin feels cold and clammy. If he had been eager maybe she would have backed off, but his reluctance is yet another spur. Why is he reluctant? Is there something about her that separates her from the girls he usually tattoos? Well, of course there must be. She can imagine her mother's comments.

It's common as muck. Only fishermen get tattooed and they want their brains examining.

Only slags have tattoos...

"Yes," she says, giving him a direct look, "I'm sure..."

"Right." Quite deliberately he raises his glass. He has compact hands and the fingers are surprisingly slender. She imagines them wielding the needle that will drill into her arm and a thrill of fear snags through her belly like a giant fish-hook.

He stands up. He's not much taller than she, but tough and wiry-looking and his jeans strain. She notices how shiny his brogues are and that strikes her as a contradiction.

They walk together up the street. It seems even hotter now and her summer dress is sticking to her.

"Where did you want it?" he asks.

She blushes again and she can feel the redness pumping up her chest and neck and she would like to run away, leap into her car and drive off without a word.

"Oh, er..." She struggles to think of something to say. "Well, I should think on the top of my left arm."

"Yer."

He unlocks the shop whilst she stands gazing down the road; there's nobody about, thank God.

When she steps into the shop, she sucks in her breath. Every wall is covered with pictures: tigers, snakes, vampires, bats, women who are half mermaid, witches, wizards, beasts - there are innumerable beasts. She sees swallows skimming over fat hearts; swallows diving above roses.

"Oo, it's amazing," she says.

He gives a grim smile. "Them's traditional," he says, pointing to the swallows and hearts, "I like something that's a bit more of a challenge..." and he looks at her.

In the middle of the room there is a pool table. She edges round it. He's making for a cubicle at the bottom of the room. She follows him into the little room. There are some black chairs, the sort you might find in an office, a small table and a rexine-covered couch. On the table, bottles of coloured fluid crowd, and there are packs of cotton wool and lint wrapped in plastic. The whole atmosphere is of something vaguely surgical - how you would imagine a backstreet abortionist's to be. Her eyes hit a naked woman whose thighs are a tropical jungle of turquoise snakes and twining plants and scarlet flowers. The patterns curl up her body to her breasts. A man, dark as a Romany, is holding her, and he too is clothed in patterns. Marilyn Monroe smiles down from her position above a steel cabinet. He notices the direction of her glance.

"I put her on a feller once... it was a brilliant tattoo... gay, he was. I'm not." He looks at her again with those strange, cold eyes. "Sit down," he says.

Her heart is thumping with fear and her mouth has gone dry. She sees this long metal lead and she's sure he'll slot the needle into it, but she doesn't want to know, or see how it's done. It's like having an injection or giving blood samples, she can never watch.

"What made you take up tattooing?"

"Good at drawing at school - did a few on me mates, then me relatives, then I was off. Most tattooists practise on pigs... I never."

"Oh... what if you do it wrong?"

"I don't... I just cover up other buggers' mistakes - I'm allus doin' that. There's loads of fellas come in that want a lass's name covering over - they've finished with her and now they want the name took off."

That's it, once the tattoo's on, you're stuck with it most likely for ever and ever. She thinks about Evan. Would she want his name tattooed on her arm? No, she can't inagine that. Maybe when she was sixteen and fell for Simon Walker... yes, she used to write his name all over, just to see how it looked. Even now there's still magic in it.

"Yer, never get a name put on."

She can tell he's speaking from experience.

"Well, what's it to be... rose or butterfly?"

"Oh, butterfly." She's panicking again and trying to stave off the moment when he'll start. The little room is stifling. He'll be touching her flesh, drilling into it.

"You get folks asking you to do all sorts."

She nods and tries to smile. He's not smiling. His pale eyes are fixed on her face. "This fella wanted a lass's name done on his dick. I wouldn't. I'm not keen on touching guys' bits. Mind you, I did two lesbians down there... had to shave 'em, you know... they had snakes coming out."

She's conscious of the couch in the corner. Her G.P. has one like that in his consulting room. She associates such couches with internal examinations - smear tests and hands gloved in plastic groping between your legs whilst you lie rigid with embarrassment. What does he do on that couch? Imagine lying there naked whilst he drills fish scales and chrysanthemum heads and peacock feather eyes into your thighs and snakes writhing out of your shaved pubic area! Just thinking about it brings her out in a wave of clamminess.

"How big do you want it?"

"Only little."

"Two inches, three?"

"Two."

He has sat down on the chair opposite and he reaches across suddenly and touches her arm.

"You'll have to have your sleeve higher than that."

She rolls up the sleeve until it won't peel back anymore. It's tight and tense in the little room with the tattooed people and Marilyn looking down. Her eyes rove over the wild territory of his arms - all that blue and green twining. She feels herself pulled down into it, out of the safe, clean world of VDUs and filing cabinets and office jokes and letters to type for important bosses. It's a dreamland, the same as the pictures in the outer room - space monsters, dragons heave themselves from primaeval mud. Evil lurks in the skulls and half-human shapes. They're the sort who flicker in and out of nightmares. All the women are Eve with the snake writhing in the crack between her legs.

She wonders what he thinks about in the morning when he wakes up and sees the weird world of his own body.

"Listen," he says, "I'm givin' you one last chance... if you don't want it doin', scarper!"

It's her opt-out... She can get up now, say she's sorry for wasting his time but she's changed her mind, and then drive back home. Evan's gone round to mow his mother's lawn, so he'll not be in for his tea until late... nobody'll know... it'll all be just like before. She'll spin them a tale in the office.

"I've told you, I know what I want."

Their eyes get entangled. His icy stare seems to come from polar regions where tons and tons of ice creak and stir and there are wide, ringing, luminous nights, utterly merciless. You would sink in there gasping until your lungs burst.

"Okay... I've had all sorts," he says, as his little fingers move about, "done a reverend once."

"What did he have?" She's not really listening to anything, but she has to ask.

"Jesus's head."

"Oh." She wonders where the reverend would have had it done. Her dress is clinging to her, she's drowning.

"I'll give you a beauty," he says and his eyes hold hers until she must look away and fix on Marilyn's golden face.

He moves the swivel chair up to where she's sitting. She's still hovering when the needle punctures her skin, and her heart gives a great bound and lurches to her throat. She wants to call out that she can't bear it, that he should stop, but she doesn't.

All the time he's working, she concentrates on Marilyn's face. It's smiling with joy like you rarely see in adults. The needle gouges and drills and hurts like hell. He's so near that she can smell his cigs and now and then a whiff of beer and a combination of his after-shave and his body. No other man gets as close to her except Evan - and even then it's not like this. She knows her arm's bleeding and she thinks if she sees the blood she'll faint. He's challenged her and she must somehow bluff it out. Her face is running with moisture.

As he works, he's quite silent. She can sense an electric current from him to her. A spell is being woven in the stabbing point of the needle. He is imposing one of his endless pictures on her. All these snakes and dragons and creeping tropical plants and the Heavy Metal skulls are intertwined with the pain. Tears come into her eyes and her throat aches. If only he would stop! She doesn't want him to see her crying but the pain is so intense she can't fathom it.

"Okay?" he asks and there's something in his tone.

"Yes," she mutters, concentrating for all she's worth on Marilyn's smiling mouth and candy-floss hair.

The needle burns and scrawls and she lolls in the chair and his little hands engrave. She remembers reading in one of her Dad's war books about Jews being tattooed in concentration camps - stamped for life.

Suddenly, when she's given up all hope of it ever ending, he stops and reaches for a pack of lint and dabs at her arm. He is scrutinising it. She turns her head slightly and sees the scar on his cheek close to. It is a pale track in the gingerish freckled skin. Their eyes meet again. You would only see someone else's face so close up in love... The ice-blue eyes are shining, turned into opals.

"There, that's it. You're done... or right... I get 'em fainting on me. Mostly the men, that is."

"Oh," she says. The spell has been broken. She feels she's returning from an unknown country.

"It'll be sore for a bit... maybe worse later on, like."

He stands up and moves away, then he returns with a mirror. "How's that, then?"

She sees the frailest, most delicate butterfly she can imagine, perching on her arm. Its wings are blue and green and traced with threads of veining. The surrounding area is puffy and red. "It's fantastic," she says.

He gives a grim smile and takes the mirror away. His buttocks are high and tight. The tropical forests invade the backs of his arms.

"You must have suffered to get all that lot done," she says. His laughter crakes.

"What do I owe you?" she asks, trusting herself to get up now and fumbling for her handbag. Her dress is sticking to her bottom and thighs.

"Pass," he says.

"Oh, no..."

"Yer."

"But..."

"Have this one on me."

"Thank you," she says as they leave the little box room. She can't think what words to use to show how pleased she is. She doesn't even know what she's feeling... it's just a tension, a strain, and her arm is stinging and throbbing and her vision is stamped with blue-green snakes and snarling dragons rearing up to belch forth red tongues of flame. And then there are his reptilian eyes that glare and never flicker and his little red moustache and the compactness of his body.

He drills her with a long look as she leaves and stumbles out to her car. It seems a different day, another year.

As she drives home to the land of 1930s semis with their bobble glass windows, brass coach-lamps and roses in front gardens, she feels she is returning from a long journey. Later she imagines that nothing has changed as she moves about the fitted kitchen rinsing lettuce and slicing cucumber and tomatoes for a salad.

It isn't until she's looking at herself in the dressing-table mirror that she can examine the butterfly and now she is overcome by a strange longing.

Evan hasn't noticed. He is busy with his nightly ritual of piling up the coins from his pocket, each in its different denomination, on the bedside table, smoothing down his suit on the hanger and putting used socks and pants in the wicker-work 'Sinbad' laundry basket.

The Betrayal

They all thought I'd gone insane when I did it; that I'd cracked up. It'll be part of the legend now that they tell everybody new.

Be very careful, there was this woman who... And their nostrils nip together with disgust and their lips curl but there's always a gleam in their eyes at the same time, because I've done the unmentionable: I've changed sides. It's more than that, though... a lot more. I've given them a glimpse of something dreadful and unbounded. You see, I didn't mess about. I didn't play on the edge, I went right over. Most of them at one time or another toy with the idea, maybe it's not even that... they just shudder and curse but behind all of it, there's curiosity.

Again and again they've asked me: why did you do it? Whatever possessed you to do it? Don't you understand the enormity of what you've done? You have betrayed a trust, You have behaved like a madwoman and a fool...

The way they all looked at me at the trial was the worst, though. Their mouths sneered and their eyes gimleted and at the same time they were undressing me. I know how they carry on in there... they talk sex, sex all day long. It's an obsession, a kind of perverseness in the screws. A long time ago they changed from being officers for me to being screws.

At the trial they asked all sorts of intimate questions, questions of a sexual nature, that I found very embarrassing. It wasn't like that at all, but they can't understand how it was.

I suppose they all thought of me as being mousy Linda Stockwell, good natured, quiet, the sort who you'd be introduced to and never remember if you met later. Ah, we haven't met, have we? I've been used to that in my life. It's the way I've dressed too - nice safe blouses and full skirts, Clarks sandals, a bit of pink lipstick but not much.

In two hours John will come and I shall have to sit facing him across the table whilst he looks into my eyes and condemns me. He thinks it was temporary insanity or something worse. I don't want to see him - I don't know why he would want to see me, unless it's to give me an ultimatum.

A year ago I was just the usual Linda Stockwell. I bet they gave me the job because I looked so middle-aged and ordinary and my particulars were right.

Stockwell, Linda. 44 years old; husband, John, 46, accountant. Two children, Sharon 14, Andy 16. Teacher.

All decent, unexceptional and safe.

But they left out something, or maybe they were watching for it. Well, I'm sure they were, only they never really expected to find it, so they didn't.

I've got a lot of time to think about what happened and I do, all day long. In fact, I can't get away from it.

It started like any other day, but it was to lead to my undoing. I'd parked my car and was being scrutinised by the navy-blue uniform in the sentry-box. He recognised me and waved. I waved back. I walked across the tarmac towards the little path that leads into the main road. Then I was approaching the Victorian red-brick frontage. I was inspected by the guys behind the glass. They smiled too. The big metal door sprang open and I drew my keys. A bevvy of screws in white shirts and navy-blue uniforms greeted me. They were coming on duty.

You should leave them morons, come and teach us instead.

They gave a suggestive laugh. I smiled and played them along.

Not likely! Do you think I'm mad!

Yes, or you'd not be workin' in here...

I crossed the yard in the wind. There's always a high wind blowing across from the estuary, even on the hottest day. I can recreate that smell of rotting fish and chemicals. Dust bowled along the forecourt and reared up. The sentry let me through another iron gate. I smiled at him.

Nice day.

Yer, you could say so...

On my left, mounds of rubbish rotted by the wall of the reception block. I unlocked the door and climbed a narrow flight of stone stairs. I was puffing by now. It was middle-age catching up, and all the breakfast rush. I'd to be in by nine. Not that anybody bothered. The screws were only too pleased if we started late.

In the admin block the security P.O. caught me.

Oh, er, Linda, could I have a word, please.

He was short and square and had gunmetal jowls and grey hair and was rather handsome.

You've got a new chap starting today on Education - an 'A' man, a lifer, Del Winters. Have a squint at his file. I want you to watch him - let us know how he behaves.

I saw the photograph of a gangster, a bank-robber, who'd shot his way out of a road-block and killed a policeman.

Winters, Del; 32 years old, divorced. Two children. Wayne 12,

Darran 11.

The mug-shot made him look savage and brooding. He'd got a fine strong neck and his eyes were defiant. Looking at his record made me feel uncomfortable. It was all about local authority homes, community homes, borstal, detention centre, prison. But all the records I have ever seen might be the same one. I nodded, then unlocked the first iron gate and the officer on the other side let me through. I saw the landings rising up in tiers round the central pit. The half-eaten bread-roll, the torn plimsoll and the underpants caught in the iron mesh that's to prevent inmates leaping or being thrown down to their death, formed a still-life. The usual sour smell hit my nostrils - it was the same as you get in here but here there's an added element - the sweet rotting stench of menstrual blood. Women's bodies seem juicier, their odour more pungent than men's.

On that first morning they brought him to the classroom door when we'd already started. I saw him first standing behind the glass, looking in. He challenged me with his angry eyes. I was determined not to be affected by him.

He swaggered in. His shoulders were braced and his arms hung by his sides but in readiness, as though he might leap to grapple an assailant. The rest watched him with respect. You don't give lifers any aggro - they've nothing to lose - anyway, most of the class were in for ten, twelve, fifteen years. It doesn't sound much... I remember thinking that. Ten years. But when you consider the length of each year and the way a minute can be an eternity, it's like thinking of forever. They'd say to me:

I panic, like... I panic, see... I'll maybe not ever come out of here alive... die in here. They're all afraid of dyin' in here...

Now I understand what they meant. I'm starting to think of it too.

He was aggressive and unco-operative. At the end of that first lesson he said to me: I suppose they've made me come here so's you could soften me up... that's it, isn't it?

I tried to keep calm, though my heart was fluttering. I didn't want to be two-faced but I could see the word typed on his record -

Psychopath...

The other men were leaving - nine chaps in blue trousers and blue and white striped shirts, who'd killed wives, girlfriends, old ladies or stolen vast sums of money.

Whatever makes you say that, I said, despising myself. I smiled into his face. His rather square, strong hands had held a gun. He'd killed a twenty-four year old policeman. I felt a bit sick. It was always the same in there: strange undercurrents, plots, machinations, and nobody knew their meaning, and the fear of violence that rippled under the surface. It haunts me still. At night I dream I'm being pursued but I don't know why.

Well, he said, I didn't ask to come on no education... didn't want it.

It's up to you... if you don't like it... but you might find it interesting.

If you say so.

He went. I saw the massiveness of his triangular back sloping to his small waist and his tight buttocks. I supposed if he weren't so ebullient, he'd die in there or become one of the druggies who spend their days on Largactil.

I didn't want to feel pity. I had to remember the demarcations - the blue uniforms were the ones who could save me from that anarchic cauldron bubbling about me.

Worse than animals, totally unscrupulous. The criminal classes... never trust a con. Once a con, always a con.

I cleaned the board and picked up my files and returned down the corridor to the gloomy little box that was the staff-room, and where the education officer had a tit calendar hanging over his desk.

Their exercise books were piled up on my table at home. I was curious to see his. I couldn't wait to find it.

Description of a scene, place, location.

His writing sloped forward and he pressed so hard on the biro that the exercise book paper had stiffened and it rattled as I turned the page.

A white beach. The blue sea lapping waves. Straw shelters where you can lie under and have iced drinks. You can run down the beach through the burning sand and plunge into the waves and the sun is a round gold ball. Theres fishermen in little boats flinging nets.

It sounded like a Bacardi advert. I was a bit disappointed. He'd be one of these playboy types who favour tropical islands where they can spend their ill-gotten gains.

We were writing again - or, rather, they were writing. They were describing a childhood experience.

His exercise book:

She was a very pretty blonde. I seen her putting all these things in a suitcase. It was one afternoon. Mam I says what are you doing. Going away she says. I didn't want her to. Then I sees this bloke drive up in a fancy yeller sports car. They was all looking out at it and the kids come out of next doors. She goes sailing down, wiggling in a white dress. We never seen her no more. Then when I was doing a twelve stretch I got this message. She was dying and wanted to see me. They never let me go, though I went in bracelets and with a load of cops to the funeral. They was all round the cemetery. My brothers was there and my dad. He couldn't keep away.

Something that changed my life

I seen these cops club this kid to death in the police cells...

He wrote. I read. I corrected for spelling and grammar, and did a big, hooking red tick at the bottom. Very sensitively described. And I wanted to be sick.

Every day I was hearing so much anguish but it didn't come out like that, it was just so many statements of what happened. You were left to draw your own conclusions.

One day he wrote:

I don't expect I shall ever come out of here alive. If you have done a cop they make sure you rot inside. I done him and I can't change anything. I'm sorry about his wife and kids. Very sorry. There's always the possibility in here of topping yourself, thank goodness.

Time passed but I didn't notice because I was watching him. He was watching me.

He told me about his life in those big houses. I knew all sorts of fragments. I was starting to dream about him, and burning to get there in the mornings. All the way in the car I'd be rigid with suspense. It didn't relax until I saw him coming through the classroom door. And then I was waiting again to hear what he'd say. I couldn't talk about him to anyone. It was my secret. When he approached the desk to speak with me, my skin tingled. In there, you were acutely aware of the positioning of people, of how many feet separated you. Everybody else knew too; everybody watched. His hand was two inches from mine for a second. I began to blush and then he looked into my face. I saw something in his eyes that made me tremble.

They'll ghost me soon, he said. I've been here a long while. They don't like you to be in one place too long.

That night I couldn't sleep. John was snoring at my side and the curtains flapped and crept in the breeze. It was a summer night and he was only on the other side of the town but it might have been on the moon. He'd go and I'd never see him again. I wouldn't be able to bear it. His grey cheeks, his strange light eyes, the square hands that would press the biro on the exercise books and hand me papers, were inescapable. They followed me everywhere. I was in a trance. Only he and I existed. Nobody else noticed anything. I was extra aware. I was always watching and waiting. The screw sat in the corridor all day long and he watched too. He stared through the glass door at what was happening in the classroom, noted the positioning of hands, who was restless, who... I knew we were all being watched.

Later that week a chap hanged himself with sheets in his cell, and I saw Del looking at me and I knew what he was thinking and I couldn't bear it.

He started writing to me in his notebook.

I shall miss you.

I found the words inside the back cover where there's a flap telling you what you may or may not write. I didn't know what to say. I kept on looking at the words. Time passed and I was dreaming. I shall miss you. I was alive like I had never been before.

In solitary you forget how to speak - that's what happened to me. You come out and you feel strange when another con addresses you.

His life had been a violent, rolling thing - a lurching from one place to another. He'd been running, hiding, enjoying, grabbing, having. Now he was wistful under the veneer, and beyond that there was sorrow. It made me look at my life. I'd always done the conventional things, never dared, always been afraid... afraid of what my parents would think, or teachers, or neighbours, or colleagues; afraid of death. From being little, Sharon and Andy had always had brilliant white ankle-socks and polished shoes and well-pressed clothes. They were nice, biddable kids. We inhabited a clean, nondescript house. I had been too afraid to live.

He wrote more letters and I drove home in an agony of suspense, wondering what they would say. Then came the note. They were ghosting him, but I could help him. Would I phone the number and collect the package? Would I carry it through in my handbag? It was up to me.

I lay sleepless. John's face was turned away from me. Would I open Del's cage and let him out?

I thought of him soaring away like some giant bird, a wild thing liberated. If I did this, it would place me forever on the other side. I looked across at John. I could see his left ear and part of his neck. His greying hair wisped against the pillow. The bald patch was growing on his skull. On the chair his underpants were neatly folded. The small change from his pocket, his keys, wallet and handkerchief were placed in careful formation on the bedside table. My children were asleep in the bedrooms across the landing. Their friends would whisper: Did you hear what she did? She...

I felt sick. My heart was bounding. My stomach churned. If I didn't do it that day, it would be too late. I didn't take risks. I was too timid. But I went at 4.15 after work and I phoned from a box in town and as I was dialling, I was gazing through the glass. Was somebody watching? Would I be arrested? A voice said, Yes? I gave the message. He told me where and when to meet him. My blouse was drenched with sweat.

The gun shocked me... oh yes, it lay in my palm. I knew what it was because I'd seen such objects on tele and on cinema screens but I'd never examined one close to. I couldn't believe in it - it was like some theatrical object - almost attractive in its menace.

I thought of all the hidden, creepy things contained in that fortress: anger, perversion, cruelty, despair, hatred. The gun was the key to Pandora's box. But was it like that? Was Del this monster? Or was all this evil the creation of the screws themselves and people like John and me: comfortable, unthinking citizens? I couldn't distinguish the victims from the torturers. Perhaps I was going mad.

I must see you about your essay, Del, I said. His back was to the door. The others were filing out. I met his eyes. I slipped him the little black object and our fingers grazed. I saw him swallow and his pupils dilated. A nerve in his cheek throbbed. I took a deep breath. He slid his right hand into his pocket.

Thank you, Linda, he said.

My skin went cold as he looked at me. Good luck, I said.

The afternoon glided by and I drove home.

That night tele was on and we were eating a ham salad at the dining table. From behind Andy's head I saw Del's face flashing up on the screen. I was irritated because I couldn't make out the whole picture. Andy was in the way. The announcer said: A dangerous criminal, Del Winters, escaped today...

I lost the rest in Sharon's voice.

I want to go to Spiders, Mum.

You're too young, John cut in.

An argument started. I wasn't listening. I was trying to catch the news. They'd set up roadblocks, but they hadn't got him. He was free. I wanted to leap in the air and shout out.

"Stockwell, you've got a visit," the screwess is saying as she unlocks me. I walk before her down the labyrinthine corridors, they're like those other corridors in that other nick - not much different.

John is sitting at the table. He's wearing his dark grey office suit and a tie I don't know.

"Linda," he says, "er, hello."

The room is full of women and children and visitors. I know the history of some of these women now: Maggie, who's killed her baby; Joan, who poisoned her drunken husband. Eddie gouges holes in her own arms...

"Hi, John... how are you?"

He's embarrassed at being here, I can tell, and his eyes are flicking about him. It must have cost him something to make this journey. His colleagues won't like it. His parents won't, either. They will have been appalled at what has happened. My own parents are dead, so I don't have to think of them. I bet he hates me.

"So, so."

"How are the kids?"

"Managing, I suppose. How have you been?"

He looks self-conscious and he can't stop glancing over at the tables where other couples are talking across at each other and some holding hands and little kids are crawling about.

"Oh, I'm all right," I say. We haven't really got anything to say to each other because my life is now in here, and his is out there, and I shall be in places like this for ten years if I live that long. I don't expect him to stand by me... why should I? Perhaps he has come today to tell me he's wanting a divorce... has found someone else and plans to remarry. That's how it goes. I've seen it so many times.

"Linda," he says suddenly, "my God, how I've missed you... I didn't know how it would be."

I find myself concentrating on him then, and I notice how grey his skin seems and his eyes are dull. He looks like someone who has been very ill.

"I'm sorry..." I say.

He puts out his hand now and grasps mine. His face is working. It is gaunt and different.

"Since this happened, I've been through hell." Now his eyes are blazing. His fingers dig into mine.

I remember how it hurt when they captured Del. He was holed up with some girlfriend. There were pictures of him and her... pictures of other girlfriends; all blonde bimbos. And then one night the three big men in dark suits came to the door and took me away. He told us, they said. John was just staring, staring.

"I could have killed you," he mutters. My fingers are squeezed between his.

I don't know what to say at the sight of so much anguish. It occurs to me then that I haven't really thought about his feelings. He has always been the same, just as I have been the same. John, the accountant, preoccupied with exactitude, with money, property... And I...? I've been bored. Nothing ever seemed to happem; I was middle-aged and I wanted to live before it was too late.

"And I've kept asking myself why, why, why the hell did you do this? At first I thought there was some mistake."

"No," I say, "there was no mistake - it was me."

"Then why?"

I take a deep breath. "I don't know." I can't pronounce the word 'love'. It hurts too much. That I appear foolish, I've no doubt... very, very foolish.

"You must have had some reason."

"At the time, I had to."

"Had to?"

I see the pain in his face.

"Was it... was it love?"

He's not the sort to talk of love. Its irrationality is too much for him.

"In a way."

"I see."

He isn't angry. We don't speak for a while. He is still holding my hand. The bell rings for the end of the visit.

"I shall wait for you, Linda... if you want me to..." He mutters it as I turn to leave. All I have time to say is thank you. I have glimpsed a generosity in him which I never expected and don't deserve, and for the first time since it happened I find that I am crying.

A Wonder of the World

Harold had been dead four months before Dots could bring herself to open the garage door. She'd intended to get his keys and swing the door up so's she could look at IT, but somehow she just couldn't. She had been pretending that it wasn't there, and might have continued to do so had it not been for her neighbour, Joyce, who didn't mess about.

"What are you going to do with Harold's car then?"

"Oh, I haven't thought about it," Dot's said, going red.

"Well, I mean to say, you can't leave it in there, it'll get spoiled. Oo, in't it lovely."

They were standing in the garage doorway staring in. There it squatted, black and shiny like some huge beetle or a hearse.

"You'd get a bomb for that, love, you want to advertise it in the Motor Mail on Friday."

"Oh, I couldn't..."

"Why ever not? I mean, Harold can't be drivin' round in heaven in it, can he!"

Dots' whole face went strawberry-coloured. How could she possibly explain; anyway, she wasn't even sure herself. It was just that THE CAR had occupied a central place in Harold's life, and therefore in hers. It wasn't something you could dismiss or enlarge upon. Joyce was wandering round it, peering in at the windows and touching the wing-mirrors.

"Pity you can't drive, love, you could have had some smashin' little runs in this."

"Well, I can."

"You never! You're a proper dark horse."

"No, well I mean Harold was the driver. It was his car... But I did pass me test - it was before you came to live here."

Joyce snorted. "You'd best get drivin' it then - it'ud be quite nice for knockin' about in - mind you, it is a bit big - eh, I'd feel like Lady Muck in one like this!"

"Yes, Harold allus liked a good sized car."

Joyce disappeared next door to get on with her vacuuming. Dots returned to look at the Rover. There wasn't a scratch on it. The chrome gleamed and there were no pits in its even sheen. Harold used to use chrome cleaner on it regularly. He'd washed it every weekend.

No use takin' it to one of them car washes - they scratch your enamel and break your aerials. Waste of money - a liability.

For Christmas one year he'd bought her a CarVac so that she could clean the interior for him, and a special tin of vinyl polish for the surrounds on the dashboard and, worse, an upholstery spray cleaner. She'd hated that because she'd invariably managed to soak the seats and Harold had got his bum wet and come in with his backside like a coconut from various bits which her cleaning had loosened.

I've never known anybody as daft as you, Dots, he'd said, call this clean!

Harold had been one of those people who knew how to do everything. All his working life he'd been an accounts clerk at Linden & McWirters. He never miscalculated. In the same way he could work out household expenditure without thinking about it. He'd also appeared to understand the mysterious money words that Dots always let her eyes leapfrog over in the paper or switched channels to avoid on T.V. One of his favourite conversation topics was routes to places.

When his mother had been alive and they'd driven down to visit her, the first hour was always taken up with: Yes, we took the M65 and then I thought we'd best make a detour. Good job we did. The M624 was single-lane traffic down to...

His Mam had listened as though he'd been recounting the most exciting adventure story and had never got round to telling him that she'd been diagnosed as having an inoperable tumor. You'd had to give Harold maximum concentration because if he'd suspected your attention was slipping, he'd sink into an impenetrable sulk.

Dots felt overwhelmed by the sight of the important-looking machine. She'd never been good at mechanical things. Harold had revelled in them. He'd bought timers for lights that she couldn't fathom. She'd receive food-mixers, lemon-squeezers and microwaves for her birthdays, whereas she liked everything quite simple - a blender was about her limit. Every now and then though, there'd be an oral exam and Harold questioned her about the machines. How was such-and-such running? Very early in the marriage she'd learnt to beam and say how grand the mixer or the ultravac was, and never mention that he'd increased her dusting acreage. In reality, the vacuum cleaner - which had an array of lights on it like a space-ship - terrified her. She'd never told him, though. The best of it was he'd thought her placid - she did have that appearance, being big and soft-faced and blond. Inside, though, she was mostly a bundle of electric wiring that was shorting.

Well, she couldn't just leave it squatting there, Joyce was right. But she couldn't sell it - that would be disloyal. He'd invested so much emotional energy in it - that was where he'd splurged his redundancy money. What would he have expected her to do? Perhaps he'd imagined it staying forever in the garage as a monument to love, like the Taj Mahal. That had always intrigued her from being a little kid - the Seven Wonders of the World. She'd thought about that beautiful young dead wife and her sorrowing husband... but this...

Dots made herself walk round it as Joyce had done. Why couldn't she drive it? There was no reason why she shouldn't. Goosepimples prickled up her arms. He'd only let her learn how to drive because she'd been all weepy and strange after Janet, their daughter, had emigrated to New Zealand.

It'll take you out of yourself... that's what you need. Only he hadn't bargained for her passing the test first time.

Passed! Examiner must have been havin' an off-day! He'd given a bark of laughter.

Could I borrow the car then, do you think - could do a big shop with it?

I'm not havin' you messin' that up - no way. You'd ruin it in five minutes.

She had only once driven in his presence, and then it had been:

Go into third now, come on, oh, my God, that was a near shave! Thought you were going to hit that parked car! Speed up, speed up, overtake... come on! You're not safe on the road. Pull over, let me drive.

Her knees had been trembling, her heart pit-pattering, and she'd been ready to faint as she'd climbed out of the driving-seat. She knew that if anything dented the immaculate bodywork Harold would never recover from it. The time when he'd come home white and strained - he'd always been a thin chap with the sort of face that made you think of stomach ulcers - but on that day she'd imagined something horrendous must have happened, a death... a road accident. He'd sat down in his chair and asked for four Disprins.

What's happened, love?

That bugger's dented me front number-plate - oh, but I'll make him pay!

If things weren't exactly right, Harold couldn't rest and he was forever at the garage.

I don't like the sound of the engine. It's racing...

He'd had an elaborate burglar alarm that pinged immediately anybody happened to approach within a few feet of the vehicle, and it frightened the life out of her.

As Dots hesitated in the garage entrance a resolve was forming in her. She would drive it, whatever the cost.

It was a frosty morning but clear, a day for action. If she didn't do

something now, she never would. She'd become more and more threatened by the menace of its perfection and she would never drive it.
There was nobody to help her. Joyce obviously thought she was stupid,
having something as valuable as that and not making any use of it. All
she had to do was drive off... but she didn't know how to reverse it.
Well, there ought to be a diagram on the gear-stick.

It seemed very quiet. The kiddies round about were at school,
Joyce was cleaning; with any luck, nobody would see her. She'd feel
such an idiot if someone she knew saw her getting stuck.

If only Harold had been there, then she wouldn't have had to
drive the monster - he wouldn't have let her; she would have been
saved. Harold had saved her from lots of things - in fact she'd never got
to do anything much on her own now that she thought of it...

She'd met him at a dance at the City Hall when she'd been seventeen, sweet seventeen and in a blue dress with a fitted bodice and a
wide swishing 'New Look' skirt. Harold, twelve years older, was thin
and intense in a grey suit with not a piece of fluff on it or a crease, and
the knot of his tie so tight and small it had shot out at a tangent from
his throat. You could have seen your face in his black lace-ups. Old
style beetle crushers, they'd been, with round toes. He was not the sort
to have crumbs on his lips or shirt-tails creeping out of his trousers. No,
he took care of what was his and never lost anything. She was different, quite the opposite... but she was forgetting... living with somebody
for a long while made it all grow muddled.

They'd become engaged two months after their first meeting.
From then on there was no more dancing - he was too jealous to permit
anyone else to get near her and he didn't like other chaps giving her the
once-over. She'd liked his possessiveness at first... later, she hadn't
been so sure... it had been like living inside a compound surrounded by
a seven foot high wall and an electrified fence, and never knowing what
was going on beyond it.

Dots sensed that what she was about to do would be somehow
very meaningful and historic. Harold had drummed into her over the
years that whatever you were undertaking, you must be wearing the
appropriate gear for it. For that reason, she put on her thick heather-
mixture tweed suit, a matching blue jumper and a little scarf, and some
flat-heeled gardening shoes - she couldn't chance any of her cuban heels
on the pedals. Normally she wore high-heels because Harold had said
they made her legs look slimmer and he couldn't bear what he called
'them clomper lads' shoes'.

When she was ready, she paused on the doorstep and looked over
the weedless square of front garden to the road beyond. It was empty.
Good. It had to be now. She took a deep breath and plodded to the car.

A grey shadow engulfed the interior of the garage. She was sweating even in the cold.

It took her a while to unlock the door. She slid into the driving-seat and examined the dashboard. Her heart was bobbing alarmingly. She turned the ignition key and the car coughed a bit but nothing happened. It had not occurred to her that it wouldn't start. Of course if it wouldn't she'd be able to postpone the confrontation - perhaps not even have it... After she'd tweaked the key four or five times and the engine had spluttered a bit, it suddenly caught. The sound, amplified by the garage, shocked her.

Now to get the reverse. She tried. There was an awful screeching. Sweat spurted from her armpits. Harold's voice thundered:

Oh, you stupid woman!

Maybe she should just leave it. But she couldn't, not with the engine droning and yelping away. It was on or bust. She remembered then about the thing called the clutch and she pressed her foot down and wiggled the gear-stick in its black rubber socket. The car shot forward towards the end of the garage and her heart gave a massive lurch. She found the brake and the car stopped. She remembered having been very good at emergency stops, in fact she'd nearly shot the instructor out of his seat. He'd been a lovely man. Sometimes his hand had come down on her knee by mistake... she'd made him very nervous.

For several seconds she sat quite still, then she restarted the car and this time managed to get it into reverse. Weaving this way and that, it crawled out into the road. Dots felt exhausted. Then she noticed that her breathing was fogging up the windscreen. She activated the windscreen wipers and they jerked across the glass making scratchy sounds. The dashboard lights blimped on. It was like being in a gauze box. She opened the window a bit and rubbed her gloves across the inside of the windscreen. Her breath was freezing on it and forming a white skin. She pressed all the buttons that looked as though they might help.

By sitting forward in her seat and staring through a clear bit just before her eyes, she could see the road ahead. She was scared, but she was rolling forward, and the fact of having got the monster moving was beginning to cheer her up. Terror alternated with something she hadn't felt for years, not since the driving instructor's hand had pressed her knee.

Where should she drive to? Maybe a quick burn up the dual carriage-way into town and then back down again and home. She was still amazed that she had managed to subdue the monster and that she was alive. This travelling along the edge experience was new to her. Inside the stockade she had never had chance to test it.

She was still congratulating herself as she took a right turn following a green light. It seemed quite a novel thing to do, and meant that she swept across the down side of the dual carriage-way.

Just as she was bowling across, windscreen wipers snarling on glass, lights blazing and fan-heater swirling icy air, the Rover was struck by something. It went into a skid, juddered, slewed over but ended upright on a pebbled verge.

Throughout, Dots - for whom the worst had now happened - was aware of certain images dizzying before her eyes in slow motion. A man's face grimaced at her. It had a look of Harold, Harold in a fury. She thought he was shaking his fist. His snazzy red number must have received the impact of the Rover, which had somehow staved in its radiator and water was cascading from it. Traffic halted spectacularly. Dots, finding herself still unhurt, opened the car door with some difficulty and got out.

"You bloody fool... you bloody fool! Why didn't you give way?"

A little man in a grey suit was bumping up and down before her brandishing his fist. Dots stood on the pebbled island feeling dazed and staring about her, and then her gaze swivelled to the Rover. It had been transformed. There it sprottled, impaled on the pebbles, a tangled mass of metal with chrome spars poking out of it. A headlamp stared at her as though in condemnation. At the sight of it, she began to laugh. She laughed until her stomach ached and the tears ran down her cheeks. The man raved on but she wasn't listening. As police cars and ambulances came wailing on the scene, Dots began to trace a feeling of mounting exhileration. Somehow she had been released. Motoring, she decided, could be very exciting, she'd suspected as much; now she knew. All she needed was a nice comfy little car, something a bit scratched that had been worn in like an old shoe. She was thinking this as two policemen strode towards her, mouths working...

Radical Surgery

Janice had been awake half the night doing Will-I-Won't-I.
Eventually she'd decided that she would have to keep the appointment.

It was important to dress up for ordeals. She'd put on her black
leggings and long-sleeved baggy black T-shirt and over this a black
jacket; then she'd hook in the antique-looking cascade earrings. For
half an hour she'd work on her face - tropical tan cheeks, blusher, purple eyeshadow. Her mouth was a big scarlet cupid's bow and her eyebrows black arcs. She finished with a blast of the 'Ciao' that Alan had
given her for her birthday.

Why was she in such a state? At her age, mother of two grown
lads, you'd have thought a little thing like this wouldn't get to her but it
did. It started her off thinking about other related things: those that
happened to you below the belt. There'd been the time at the Family
Planning Clinic when she'd had to wait on a chair in a corridor to see
the doctor and all these men in suits had gone plonking past on their
way upstairs to some offices. They'd ogled at her because they knew
what she was waiting for. She felt like pulling her tongue out at them
and waggling her ears - Seen enough, then! - but of course she hadn't.

Then there was THE SMEAR. It was useful at work if you needed
time off for some reason. When she'd been doing shop-work and she'd
wanted a couple of hours for Christmas shopping once, she'd whispered
in the manager's ear:

I've got to go and have a smear, Mr Burgoin.

At the sound of the word smear he had gone red, averted his gaze,
cleared his throat and said, Yes, yes... and shot away as fast as he
could.

That, of course, was a positive use of smear, but the actual proce-
dure itself was pretty much like the Family Planning Clinic.

Even the having of babies and the business of knickers-off and a
different feller's hand groping about inside you each time you attended
the antenatal clinic couldn't prepare you for all the other close encounters, though it did help in some way because you stopped thinking of
yourself as Sleeping Beauty. No Sleeping Beauty ever lay on a couch
with her bum in the air and her legs in stirrups and crowds of stringy-

necked youths peering interestedly at her shaven crotch.

One way of getting yourself to accept anything spooky that was pending was to run through the catalogue of gruesome encounters which you had already survived. This was a technique Janice had mastered several years ago.

During the brisk toddle to the hospital, she tried them all out in preparation for this new encounter. Now why should it be any different from the others? Why did it threaten to be worse?

Well, all the others had been below the belt business - this was above it. This was tangled up with all sorts of things: Page 3 girls; Men Only; Penthouse; Mayfair - these spreads with topless lasses, pouting and beaming and sulking as they thrust their sellotape-assisted cones at the camera.

It started early on and perhaps that was why it stuck. She remembered noticing when she was about eleven, and around the same time she 'started', that her front was budding. All the girls in her class had been straight up and down but there she was with this wobbly front. She didn't like to be lolloping up and down when she ran. And there'd been the times at the swimming baths when she'd noticed these lads practically drowning because they wouldn't stop ogling at this lass with massive boobs, and she'd thought, If I get like that, I'll die. They'd been a law unto themselves though, and they'd grown and grown.

By the time she was sixteen, it was becoming a definite advantage to be a 36C cup. The skinny black polo necks and the long circular skirts and pumps had launched her into romance.

You've gor a smashin' figure, Ken had told her when they were jiving in the Locarno to 'Rock Around the Clock'.

Yes, at seventeen, sweet seventeen, she'd had this fantastic figure - the boobs were her passport to men. That was what all these fellers looked for; they concentrated on measurements - funny that women didn't gloat about men's chest sizes...

Oh, he's a forty-two... or Oh, he's a pigeon-chested thirty-two...

They never seemed to fix on details in the same way men did. At school the lads had all seemed better at figures than the lasses... perhaps that was why?

For years and years she'd been fastening herself into what felt like an iron lung - that was when there'd first been that bra style with the underwired cups. They pushed your boobs up so that they looked like giant cup-cakes or canapés. When she'd worn a strapless dance dress, it had been even worse. She'd been encased in a corselet which meant that she mustn't eat until the evening was over.

But it all came back to your boobs... there was no escaping it. They were supposed to be the big allure... and if you hadn't any, what then? The thought was too horrific to explore.

The hospital looked like a prison. It was built of orange brick and had square towers. She had to cross an asphalted yard where there were lots of double yellow lines and neat little parking oblongs that had 'consultant' written on them in white. Parking spaces, like lavatories and doctors' couches, are places where you get to know your proper position in life. Wherever she'd worked, the manager had always had his own toilet, his own key and his own parking space.

An arrow pointed to Radiography and, in smaller print, Mammography.

A queasiness rumbled in her stomach and everything seemed very far away: the parked ambulances; the consultants' BMWs and Volvos, and the yellow tramlines outlining all the corners. It was like the school yard - skipping, and her new boobs going bang, bang as she leapt, and the lads calling: Oo, let's feel your knockers! She would have liked to have vanished into thin air.

She went through the door marked Mammography. A secretarial-looking woman was sitting at a desk writing something. She glanced up and smiled. It was one of those I-have-been-trained-to-mummy-you smiles.

"Have you an appointment?"

Should she say no and flee?

"Yes, Hewit... Janice."

"Oh yes, Mrs Hewit. Like to take a seat in the waiting-room just round the corner. Nurse will call you when it's your turn... thank you."

The waiting-room had mushroom-coloured shag-pile carpets and pink and beige and green flowered wallpaper and pale-green curtains, and there was a picture on the wall of a thatched cottage and a country garden. Easy chairs clustered around a glass-topped coffee-table.

At the doctor's you'd normally found a pile of dog-eared 'Woman' and 'Woman's Owns' or 'Woman's Weeklies' and some 'Beezers' and 'Dandys' for the kids. But here it was 'Homes and Gardens' and 'Good Housekeeping' and 'Country Life': mags with real thick glossy pages, showing dining-rooms the size of her entire house, and Mrs Taylor Ridgeway's conservatory which looked like the botanical garden she'd once seen on a trip to London. Very nice.

Janice was unnerved by the quietness and the well-bred cosiness everywhere. She studied the country garden picture. There'd be no yellow mould splodges on the rose leaves in such a garden; no rampant twitch grass with white roots like drawn wisdom teeth; no dry rot in the cottage; nothing nasty like adultery or bad breath. This great show of pinks and beiges and pale greens was intended to make you feel it was all right; lull you into false comfiness.

A brass plaque had been affixed to the wall near the picture:

This Unit was paid for by public subscription and opened by the Princess Royal in September 1991.

All these things were supposed to be protecting you, by spotting areas where the rot had set in. Well, what if she had got this lump somewhere inside her eating her away? It must be like the black spot her Dad used to find on his tomatoes - there they'd be: glossy, orangy globes, weighing down the plants almost. The greenhouse would be full of their fragrance... but then he'd discover the black dots and when you cut the tomatoes open, you'd see the patch of badness extended right inside. Yes, what if... They said there must be lumps you couldn't feel with your fingers they were so small. You were told to search for them. The thing about feeling for lumps was, you might not be able to decide what were considered to be lumps and what not.

This business about there being something you might think you perhaps could have but didn't know you already had, was like when you suspected your husband was having it off with someone but you didn't know for sure. You'd be looking at his trousers folded over the chair and thinking - Will there be a letter in his pocket; will there be something that'll tell me the truth? Do I really want to know? Of course I must find out...

It had been like that with Ken after she'd had Howard. She'd known he was different but she couldn't make out how. He'd been kind of lit up. She'd been looking everywhere for signs; sniffing his clothes - was that perfume? - going through his pockets, scrutinising his Y-fronts... always wanting the truth but dreading it, thinking that here was somebody she didn't know: a stranger. Had she been asleep and missed something vital whilst she was pregnant and later, nursing Howard - all those nappies and bottles and broken nights and exhaustion. And one day she'd heard it from her neighbour:

When you was in hospital, love, having the bairn, he brought that friend of yours, Christine, back here... thought you ought to know, like...

Another woman was coming in. She looked a real snooty cow: tweed suit, pink jumper, beige shoes for the wider foot, real middle-aged gear. Her hair was going grey and permed. She sat down and snapped her beige handbag open. It was one of these square leather ones with two handles, expensive and fuddy-duddy as well - no style, just boring. She took out a little white handkerchief, unfolded it and blew her nose and refolded it, all in a real finicky way. Fancy still using real handkerchiefs - she'd given that up years ago. Next the woman got her specs out and reached for a mag, but she didn't look at it for long. Then her eyes dodged about. Janice met them and made herself smile.

"Seems like they must be having a tea break."

"Oh, er, do you think so?"

She had a posh voice.

"Reckon so - I've been in here for ages."

"They said it would take about twenty minutes - I hope it's not going to be a long wait. I wouldn't have come if I'd thought."

She was all set to witter on indefinitely about it. Janice knew her sort. She saw them all the time in the pub where she was bar-maiding. They were the ones who'd expect to be served first even if they were at the back.

"It's always a long wait in these places."

"Yes."

"Have you been before?"

"No."

"I didn't want to come," Janice confessed.

"No," the woman said, "I can't say that I did."

Janice thought she looked quite human as she made that admission.

"If I've got something, I don't know..." All of a sudden her face crumpled up and she snapped her bag open again and started rummaging for the handkerchief.

"What's up?" Janice asked.

"I don't want to burden you."

"Oh, feel free - folks are allus telling me things."

"It's just..." She was dabbing at her nose again. "I think my husband's having an affair - I mean, I'm not young anymore... we've been married thirty years..."

"Yer..." Janice found she was having to stare at her own hands because the woman seemed so naked that it hurt to look at her.

"I was driving here... you see I'd normally be teaching at this time... and as I came up to some traffic lights, I saw Ivor, my husband, with this young woman beside him... I mean she was looking into his face... it was..." She broke off, struggling for control. "It was her face I could see."

"Yer," Janice said, "and what are you going to do then like?"

"I haven't thought that far, my head's whirling. I can't stop seeing that picture. She was so young... about eighteen, I'd guess... younger than our daughters."

Janice could just imagine that bloody Ivor - he'd be one of these big fellers with a lot of thick grey hair and he'd be suited up and discreetly smelling of French after-shave and he'd have a heavy gold signet ring on his little finger - the sort of chap who reeks of power. And poor old Mrs Ivor must have spent thirty years trotting off to the drycleaners with his suits and jamming his frolic-stained underpants into the washing-machine and cooking little treats for him.

"Of course it might not be anything."

"No," the woman said, "but I think it is."

Janice was shooting back over the old ground... what if they found a shadow on that x-ray and the brown letter came from the Health Authority? What if it said: Would you please come back for further tests? And then... All that Page 3ing and the Playboy number belonged somewhere else. They were about tricky games that you could only play if you were eighteen and hadn't a mark on you, but a lot of people believed that was what it was all about...

As a woman, your body zipped through all these stages: you were a kid one minute and you knew nothing but you were excited and scared of what you were becoming with all this periods and breasts and what not. You spent ages thinking your bum was sticking out or your boobs were too big or too little and your legs too fat or scrawny. You didn't know you were really at your best, as near perfection as you'd ever be - only Sugar Daddies could see that and your Mam who was frightened for you. And then there were all the adventures and the next thing you were pregnant and that newness was ruined: silver snail-tracks on your belly and thighs and your boobs took a nose-dive and ended up round your waist. It had gone. After that it was just a case of maintaining an illusion and making adjustments for your sagging jaw and your crow's feet and your veins; just generally keeping the show on the road, and she'd grown adept at it. They got you having all these tests for bone-thinning and breast cancer and cervical cancer... you name it. Your next stage was the menopause - pause in men - another great unknown and unmentionable. Nobody could tell you what happened then. It was rumoured some went dotty; had hot flushes; dried up; their men cleared off. They made you think it was a complete disaster area and that you became invisible thereafter. Then bang, you'd zoomed through it; you were floating. The hot flushes were quite nice once you'd got the hang of 'em; you saved a bomb on towels and scarpering males... well...

"And I keep thinking," Mrs Ivor was saying, "if I ended up with something wrong as well... you know... I'd never be able to live with him anymore. I couldn't bear it."

"All I can say, if you think he's that bad, you'd be well rid."

The woman was looking at her with very wide-open eyes. If she coloured her hair and got out of those dead-leg clothes, she could look quite attractive.

"But..."

"Leave him to it... you don't have to suffer... in a bit he'll get waterworks trouble and then she'll be off... she won't want to be doing bath-chair service. That's how it goes..."

"You do say some things!" the woman was almost smiling.

"Yer, well when you've been married and divorced and been about a bit you get to see how it works."

"Mrs Hewit?" This young woman in a navy-blue uniform was calling.

"That's it - listen, I work at the Angel - in the bar. Come in and have a drink."

"Well, thank you - I'm Alison by the way."

All the time Janice was having her breasts squeezed and pressed into the machine by a little radiographer who looked about sixteen, she kept thinking about Alison and the nasty Ivor - yes, if it was her she'd definitely opt for radical surgery. Once she'd got rid of that bugger she could start living again.

"Well, that's it, thank you, Mrs Hewit. You should hear from us in about two weeks time."

"Thanks, love," Janice said.

Later that evening, up to her neck in bubble-bath, she stretched in the delightfully warm water and watched the lace of bubbles slithering above her submerged limbs, and she felt a great glow of satisfaction. After this luxurious routine she would be slipping into her candlewick dressing-gown, popping her chicken tikka into the microwave and opening her can of lager. Then she would sprottle before the tele, watching the Clint Eastwood video that Howard had brought for her. Of course she'd have her feet up on the pouffe, gas fire blazing and the lager at her elbow. This definitely beat an evening out with Alan and having her little toes nipped as she tottered in her stilettos, and her earhole battered by tales of his wife's dumbness and his possible redundancy in an office coup. She'd been supposed to be spending an evening/night with him, it being her day off and his wife having gone to see her folks in Manchester for a few days, but she'd rung him at his office to say she didn't feel well enough after the hospital visit. It had just been like saying the word 'smear'. He had clammed up immediately.

As she munched her chicken tikka and forked up the rice, she concentrated on Clint's real sensitive face - it was rough and battered but it did look honest...

Out of the Question

Nicky had never really liked Granger. He was the sort of kid who could be nice one minute if you were on your own with him, and gruesome if his cronies happened to be about. Of course he came first in the cross-country and he was a champion soccer player. He trained with a sports club and was in the County's junior team. Being big and with his handsome face, he knew how to turn on the charm with adults. When he smiled, he looked sincere and they always believed what he said.

It irritated Nicky that he would find himself smiling and trying to be pleasant with Granger - sucking up to him almost - when he didn't want to be doing that at all. He didn't know why he did it and he wished he could stop. Even when Granger was being friendly, Nicky couldn't trust him and it made him uneasy the whole time. Nobody who had any sense would get the wrong side of Granger. Everybody else in the class was known by their first names, all except Granger. That alone made him stand out.

At lessons he was average but nobody bothered about that; anyway he could get by all right.

On this particular afternoon Mr Williams had said they were to have a debate: Capital Punishment should be re-introduced.

"Now then, who's going to speak for the motion?" His eyes leap-frogged about the room.

"What's that about, Sir?" Granger asked.

"Whether hanging should be re-introduced, Michael."

"Oh, I will."

"Good."

Mr Williams often had difficulty controlling them. Granger and co. would send missiles zipping about the room when Mr Williams' back was turned. By the time he'd shot round, they would be studying their exercise-books. But Nicky got the impression that the teacher suspected what was going on and so he'd give Granger jobs to do. Granger was the smooth-faced smiling gobby who spoke for the class.

It was very hot in the room and Nicky sweated in his school shirt and V-necked sweater.

Don't start flinging your clothes off the minute there's a bit of sun, his mother warned, you'll end up poorly with your chest. His chest, he felt, was like his Dad's car that might break down at any minute. It made him nervous. He didn't want to be ill and stuck in bed, coughing up gobs of gozz. Other kids could go wandering round without their coats on in the middle of winter. Granger only ever wore T-shirts and he never got a cold. If you passed through town on a Saturday night there'd be all these kids in their white shirts and with their sleeves rolled up even when there was snow on the ground.

Nicky sat doodling on a page at the back of his English book, then he put his biro down. He was dreaming a bit and humming under his breath. It was 'Public Enemy'. He loved the insistent chanting and the sirens pipping in and the zizzy-zizzy of the turn-tables. He was a rapper whining and screeching out his message and his fingers tapped the beat under the desk.

"Nicholas Davison, what's the matter with you? Aren't you with us, then?"

All the heads shot round and the laughter gusted. Nicky often wondered why a bunch of kids seemed to enjoy picking on one poor bugger. You'd be okay, well-in all round, or so it seemed - though he invariably felt that his position was precarious - and then if anybody pointed out a peculiarity, you'd be finished. The safest thing was to be exactly like everyone else. He never quite succeeded, and he didn't know why. But at the same time, there was this part of him that didn't want to be just like everyone else. Why should he have to go their way?

For one thing, Granger was a 'Trendy'. He followed the music in the Charts and wore normal jeans out of school - oh, they'd be expensive - 501s or Lees - big jackets and 'Adidas' trainers with the tongues sticking up. Nicky didn't want to be like that; he fancied baseball caps and great wafter jeans and layers of T-shirts and flappy garments.

"Are you taking part in this debate then, Nicholas?" Mr Williams was regarding him with a sarcastic smile and a raised eyebrow. "Or have you decided to dream on?" There was another burst of laughter. In fact it ballooned into a great bellow and ranted out of hand so that Mr Williams had to thump his desk.

"Pack it in there, calm down! That's enough. We've wasted enough time as it is. Come on!"

Nicky sat there and thought about hanging. A lot of the time in class he was bored and drifting, but this clawed at his attention. Hanging. He imagined the rope round his neck, drawing tighter and tighter and his eyes popping. They pushed you through a trap-door he'd heard. In America they gave people injections that sometimes didn't kill them. The electric chair. Imagine sitting in a chair that made your heart judder until it stopped. Just thinking about it all caused his heart to bump and blunder.

"I'll do the opposition," he mumbled.

"What are you saying, Nicholas?"

"Put me on the other side, Sir."

"I think all them who do a murder should have capital punishment - particularly child murderers and sex cases. It says in the Bible an eye for an eye a tooth for a tooth." Granger dried up then and frowned at Nicky.

"Come on, Nicholas!" Mr Williams blustered. Nicky got the feeling that maybe Mr W was scared of Granger. He never hassled him when it was his turn.

"Well, I don't think it does any good hanging people. I mean if you kill 'em you're only making things worse - and anyway they'll never get any better if you just kill 'em. They might not have done it either."

It all seemed quite straightforward in his head but he couldn't get the words out. What he said wasn't what he thought. When he thought of the word 'hanging', it made him feel sick. He'd heard about all these guys on Death Row in America and he couldn't imagine anything worse.

"I mean," he began again, "when you kill somebody you just do it like that but if you have hanging, it means it's kind of all planned out - and anyway what about the ones who have to hang the criminals?"

"You want to keep sex cases alive, and murderers?" Granger was staring at him and his eyes had widened into hard disbelief. "They want exterminating."

Things were hotting up. Granger's cronies shouted "'Ere, 'ere!"

"Why should the rate-payers have to pay to feed 'em in prison? It'ud be a lot cheaper if they was to hang 'em. And anyway when they get out, they only do it again."

"But how would you feel if you'd done it and it was *you* they were going to hang? Or if you hadn't done it, but they thought you had?"

For a few seconds Granger stared across at him. Why didn't it occur to him that he could just as easy be the criminal as anyone else? Nicky always felt that he himself might be the one. He puzzled about this, whilst waiting for Granger to answer.

"Well, I wouldn't do owt like that anyway."

The question had stirred him up because he pulled a face.

"You don't know," Nicky kept on.

"Don't be daft, I'm not mental. Sex cases and terrorists want hangin'."

A general uproar threatened and Nicky could hear the rest swapping favourite murders.

"And what about that feller who killed them kids in that playground? My Dad says they should have strung him up - and my Mam says they should do experiments on him like wot they do on animals."

"We don't seem to be getting anywhere with this," Mr Williams said. "What's happened to the debate? Come on, settle down lads! Nicholas, have you anything further to say?"

Nicky struggled to think of something. Basically he just felt hanging wasn't the right thing to do. He was always on the side of the Trojans in the Greek and Trojan war. Any loser excited his sympathy and he couldn't help putting himself in the place of the guy who was getting ready to drop through the trap-door.

"I just think it's wrong."

"They're vermin and want exterminatin'." Granger was glaring across at Nicky.

"No!" Nicky almost shouted. He could feel himself preparing for the drop. He hated it; he hated the way Granger had no mercy in him and kept on repeating the same things over and over with hard eyes; and all Granger's mates were backing him up and sneering. Lost causes - why must he be pulled in his guts to follow lost causes? Why couldn't he feel the same moral superiority that they did? Was he the weirdo they thought him to be?

"He's only against hangin' because of his Dad."

"What are you saying, Michael?"

"Nothing, Sir," Granger said.

Nicky felt his cheeks grow hot. His heart was racing. What was Granger on about?

"What do you mean?" Nicky asked. The other lads had fallen silent and were earwigging like mad.

"My Dad says yours is a criminal - a murderer."

"Michael," Mr Williams said, "it isn't a good idea to be making such allegations. Anyway, let's have the vote. Those in favour of the motion?"

That was almost everybody, Nicky wanted to cry but he swallowed hard and kept his eyes down and thought of the 'Public Enemy' tape he'd got at home. Why had Granger said that about his Dad? Granger's Dad was a prison officer and that gave him authority to talk about prisoners and the sorts of things they'd done. Granger often described rapes and murders, that his father had told of, with an excited face.

And this feller had cut the tits off of this lass - yer, he had.

Go on, he never...

He did - cross my heart and hope to die. You can ask my Dad if you don't believe me.

The bell shrilled for the end of afternoon school. Nicky hoped that

Granger and his mates wouldn't try to stop him. He wanted to get away as fast as he could to think. What was this about his Dad?

Granger was in the middle of a group near the school entrance. He was telling something. They all looked round at his approach and sniggered. Again Nicky felt he would cry but he controlled it until he was out in the road and then he found tears plopping down his cheeks. The wind was blowing and he let it whip his skin dry. He felt weak, as though all the life had been wrung out of him.

He was thinking about his Dad. When he arrived home from work, his hair was sometimes frosted with paint. He'd have a weird white strand sticking up on the top of his head, or else he might have white in his nails and there'd be a combined smell of paint and cigs on him and the nice fuggy smell from under his arms. That under-arm scent meant Dad. He liked it better than the spicy perfume of his after-shave lotion when he was off out to the pub with Mam, or going to the club.

Dad organised special treats - he always had. He was different from Mam. She was sensible; she warned; she had no time - the shop-ping chivvied, her and the cleaning. It was always: If you do that, you'll be ill, or get fat, or get bad teeth, or mess up your clothes. Dad didn't care. They'd be at the cinema, plonked right in the middle, 'Cornettos' stuck in their hands, licking away at the sweet white ice cream and chomping on the brittle shell of chocolate. Pirates shook their fists and brandished their sabres; or the great shining figure of the 'Terminator' rose up on the screen. One time they'd scrunched down hot-dogs and sucked up orange through straws, all whilst the figures flashed up, and it was so exciting you just wanted it never to stop. But if it did get bad, Dad was there to hang onto and lean against.

Whatever Dad did was magic - but he had to be in the mood. If he was in a bad temper, it was best to keep clear of him.

There was that time when Uncle Gary turned up. He hadn't ever met Uncle Gary before and for some reason Dad wasn't pleased to see him. Uncle Gary rattled on. Dad just stared at him and his eyes scrunched up into slits so that you could hardly see the chestnut colour and his mouth pulled into a line. Nicky listened all the time, trying to tell what must have happened, but it was like switching on tele when the play was halfway through.

Dad and Uncle Gary went out. Mam was very smiley, which meant she was uneasy as well. There was something scratchy and dan-gerous. Next morning he asked:

Where's Uncle Gary, Mam? I thought he was staying over?

Oh, he's gone back home now, love.

In the car, his Dad had to be first. If other drivers went slow or dodged about, Dad would curse and accelerate and his mouth would turn into a letter-box slit and his eyes squeeze up and glare.

Once a fellow pipped. Dad gave chase. He was a young chap in a new Ford and Dad's face turned white, his hands clamped the steering wheel and Nicky knew that his Dad had only one thought in his mind. Nicky was praying: Please God, don't let Dad catch him... let our car break down.

The Ford shot away and they went home and Dad complained about the dinner and Nicky kept quiet, waiting for the blackness to pass.

Somewhere in Dad there was all this hand-wrenching, eye-scrunching, mouth-letter-box fury. It never came right out, but it could. Nicky sensed that if it once did, anything could happen. Was this the one who Granger said was a criminal, a murderer? They'd all keep on about it now. Murderer - like those guys on Death Row. But it couldn't be true. It was just Granger doing his usual gobby number. What about Granger's Dad? His Dad had fetched him after they'd been on the school trip to 'Flamingo Land'. He was like Granger only bigger. He wore a leather jacket; a thick gold identity bracelet drooped on his wrist and he had a gold chain round his neck and a lot of knuckle-duster rings spiked his fingers. Granger's Dad would be the same sort as Granger- a gobby.

Nicky wondered how he could put the question: Er, Dad, are you a murderer? Dad, Granger says you're a murderer, is it true?

Thinking of it brought the sick feeling on again. He dawdled on the road home and stared in at the shop windows. At the newsagents he could see the magazine racks and the greeting-card stands and the mounds of sugared almonds and mint imperials or wrapped toffees waiting for you to take the small scoop and dribble the sweets into the white bags that were sprinkled with red hearts. Usually he would have looked longingly in their direction - but not today. They were no longer interesting; nor was the hairdresser's where you'd see the owner's scarlet Porsche squatting by the kerb and the whiz-kid himself with his designer pony-tail flourishing his scissors as he cut and shaped some woman's hair. The perfect faces on the big window ads for conditioners and shampoos leered out at him. Everything was going on at a distance behind thick glass.

They lived in a terrace which faced onto the main road and Nicky had his own latch-key. He let himself in. The house was silent and he didn't like it. He switched on the tele in the front room and then went into the kitchen. The silence still persisted although he could hear the television voice talking away. A shadow crossed the whirly patterns in the kitchen door and he jumped. It was only the branch of next-door's tree.

He took two slices of 'Wonderloaf' from the plastic bag and stuck them in the toaster.

If Dad had murdered someone then who would it have been? You could be murdered at any time; someone could be lurking upstairs who would come creeping down and hack you to death with a penknife or squeeze your throat until you choked to death. On tele and in the movies people were killing one another every day. According to what you heard, it seemed to be some people's chief preoccupation. But why would someone kill you, if you hadn't harmed them? What would be the point?

When the toast popped up he jumped with shock and sweated, then he sat down at the kitchen table and spread marg on the brown squares and a thick layer of raspberry jam.

So, when his Dad came in, he'd ask: Dad, Granger, this kid in our class, says you're a murderer.

What would happen if his Dad said - Yes, lad, I am... I killed this mate of mine... ?

Just before six o'clock his Mam and Dad both arrived home from work within minutes of each other. His Mam put some meat pies in the oven and his Dad went to wash his hands; later he sat down in the front room with the evening paper. Nicky was finishing off his Maths homework, but he couldn't concentrate. He stared over at his Dad whose face was hidden behind the paper. He studied the top of his head where the hair was thinning and flecked with grey. The deep crooked line running across his forehead had eased out.

All of a sudden his Dad looked up and smiled. "What's up, son, have I got paint on me hair?"

"No, Dad." Nicky gazed at his father's familiar toffee-coloured eyes that were smiling at him, and he felt like crying, because it occurred to him that one day his Dad would die and he didn't want him to; he wanted him to live forever. "I'm stuck with me homework, that's all..."

"Keep tryin'," his Dad muttered, and the paper rose again.

There was no point in asking the question, Nicky decided, because he didn't want to know the answer anymore.

The Eternal Triangle

After several months of denture-gnashing and moping indoors following the departure of her toy-boy, Jason, Beryl had got up one morning, put on her tropical-tan cheeks, spiked up her eye-lashes, rubied her lips, and started on her new life. Somehow she must come to terms with her awful loneliness: first Billy had died on her and now Jason had scarpered.

She'd been well aware of what they were all saying at the Mayfair Bingo and in the Crown and round about.

Oh well, serves her right - that Beryl's a right goer... she's had it comin'. Old enough to be the lad's nana... yer, did you see, her husband not in his coffin and she's shakin' a leg...

Well, it had been grand while it lasted - such a lovely lad. She'd fallen for him because of his mohican - all those magnificient scarlet spines. When she'd caught sight of his profile at first, it had reminded her of a warrior's head; the sort she'd seen in her history books as a kid - a roman legionary perhaps; someone with a bright sword and mighty muscles. All her life she'd had this yearning for the exotic; something just a bit different. And then he'd had it all lopped off and ever since he'd looked like a bar of white Vinolia baby soap. Of course him not being able to go out in bad weather or if the wind blew had been a bit limiting and it had been embarrassing when he'd worn the plastic bag over his head.

On that first day out an amazing thing had happened. Just as she was reaching for a tin of pilchards on the supermarket shelves a voice had murmured: Allow me!

Bony fingers had tweaked up the round tin and placed it in her hand. Her heart had fluttered.

Ta very much.

Know who I am?

It's, er, Stan.

Now Stan Draper was a guy she'd known of all her life but not seen since she was about fifteen. They'd gone to the same school, though he'd been a bit older; rather a smart-Alec if she remembered. He'd had a D.A. - a beauty - and his hair had formed a quaff at the front, like Tony Curtis's had. Every time he passed a shop window, he'd be whipping his comb out of his back pocket and flicking the sides back and then patting them to make sure they were fitting together. All the lasses'ud be staring at his long grey drain-pipe legs and his maroon brothel creepers.

The swinger of those times had metamorphosed into a tall skinny bloke who was belted into a grey Norwegian army surplus gabardine raincoat and had a flat cap mushrooming on his head.

You living round here, like, Beryl?

Yer, just across there... She'd gestured towards the front of the shop.

How about a cuppa then?

That was a bit cheeky, she'd thought, but still... might as well. She was still trying to match the blond D.A. and the massive maroon shoes with this rather dodgy-looking chap peering out of his specs at her in an intense sort of way.

Why not? Wait while I've got me bits and pieces.

He'd hung about, hovering by her, so that she'd forgottn to buy the lav cleaner and the crumpets for tea.

From then on, Stan began to besiege her. Blue boxes of Cadbury's Roses or Quality Street appeared on the doorstep with little notes saying he was just passing. Once she found a dead fish - a plaice with that funny brindled skin and yellow spots, sandwiched between sopping sheets of newspaper and reposing on the lintel.

Something for your tea, the note had said. He didn't know of course that she never had cared for plaice.

Whilst all this was going on, one afternoon in the deep marigold gloom of the bingo palace, she'd run into Eddie. There was one room given over totally to fruit machines, and when Beryl was feeling low or in need of a swift burst of rejuvenation, she would pop in there first before the serious bingo started. It was exciting to hear the singing of the machines and the full-throated whirring which might end in the thrilling sound of ten ps pinging down in silver-coloured rain from the metal chute.

On this afternoon she'd been concentrating on the line-up of fruit: a bright yellow banana, a red plum, an orange, a green apple. You had to try for a single row of the same fruit. She was thumping the nudge-button when a soft voice said:

Hello, Beryl, how're you doing?

Oh, Eddie, yer, just a minute...

If she could just get that last banana up!

The pictures revolved; that machine crooned and then bang, a plum shot up, the line was spoiled - end of singing. Zonk. The light blinked malevolently.

Beryl was annoyed. She didn't like people talking to her when she was playing the machines. It was like somebody watching you when you were shopping or cooking...

Eddie had always been around too, as long as she could remember but a lot of the time he hadn't been at large as his life had been dominated by his Mam.

How's your Mam? Beryl had asked because it was so unusual to find Eddie on the loose in there.

Mam, it seemed, had finally pegged it, and then he'd been made redundant at the frozen food place and so he was floating free.

She'd always liked Eddie. Nowadays his hair was grey but there was still quite a lot of it and it curled into the collar of his mac, and in that light it had the tarnished glow of old smokers' moustaches.

I'm at a bit of a loose end like, he'd said. She could see he wasn't really interested in the machines, whereas she was. She just liked having a flutter. Of course you got a lot of people in the bingo who'd be there all day. It was the company as well. You could sit in the main hall that used to be the cinema, play bingo and buy sandwiches and drinks from the bar and you might have been anywhere - Costa-you-know. With the light always being that brassy colour even in the middle of the day, it was like a perpetual night out.

Eddie had bought her a coffee but when she was trying to listen to the caller - One and one, legs eleven; nine and six, ninety-six... - he would keep on telling her about when his Mam went.

She was took at night, real late... and I'm tellin' you...

Two fat ladies, eighty-eight.

Somebody called and everything stopped and the lights winked and Beryl found she was sweating. Everybody was glaring at one another.

Eddie had a story. She'd heard it from someone ages ago. One time he'd nearly escaped from his Mam and that was when he went to live with this lass, Eunice. It didn't last long because Eunice ran off with another chap; she couldn't stand being stuck with his Mam as well. After that he gave up and stayed put with the old lady. But if Beryl had ever glimpsed him, she'd always thought - Poor bugger!

It was impossible not to accept when Eddie asked her round for a coffee after the bingo. Well, it ended up being tea at his Mam's.

I allus think of it as Mam's, he'd said.

The house was spotless: chairback covers lined up, china cabinet gleaming, carpets vacuumed. He still took off his shoes at the front door. It was clear he knew all about shopping and baking cakes - she ate a piece of jam sponge and it was honey-coloured and so light you didn't need to chew it. She'd expected goo in the middle or burnt bits...

His eyes were grey and they reminded her of striped cats; all of him was feline; sort of soft, elastic and pouncy. He made her think of her cat, Big Striper, who settled on men's knees like a huge and breathing fungus and would then stretch his paws and unsheath his hooks so that they snagged flesh. He used to do that to Jason, but generally Jason's jeans took the brunt of the spiking. Of course he'd been Billy her late husband's cat.

What the bairns, Nicky and Stu, didn't know was that she was now suddenly in the middle of a very intricate social life. They had their own households. Nicky was married and had two kiddies, and Stu had lived with a couple of birds - not simultaneously - but it hadn't come to anything, so now he was on his own. They assumed she was fading away from loneliness and disappointment.

Mam, we want you to have a special treat, they'd said. We was thinking of a party.

That was how she came to be throwing a party at her house to celebrate her sixtieth birthday.

Stu arrived first at six o'clock. He was on Social, so he took life at a leisurely pace.

"Many happy returns, Mam," he said. He'd got his hair gelled back and looked quite bonny in his 501s and his baggy white shirt. She liked his gold hoop earring. A nose jewel would have suited him too, like Jason used to have before he lost his mohican, but Stu wouldn't go that far: he had limits. She remembered him screaming when she'd tried to get him into trendy gear - red jeans and a red and yellow striped T-shirt. In fact they'd had a battle in the middle of Boyes's. Still...

"Here you are!" and he handed her a gift-wrapped box. "Just to cheer you up a bit."

"Very nice of you, Stu." It was a pot figurine. A bit more dusting, she registered.

Hard on his heels came Stan. He was wearing a dark suit with lapels like rabbits' ears. Beryl noticed how Stu eyed him suspiciously.

"Stan, this is my lad, Stu."

"Stu, Stan's a friend of mine."

"Oh."

Stan's prezzie was clearly jewellery from the size of the box.

In a short time the house was full of people balancing plates in their hands and cups of tea. Eddie hung about looking uncomfortable near the door.

Beryl realised that Nicky and Stu didn't approve of her two men friends.

"Who're *they*?" Nicky whispered in Eddie's hearing.

"Oh, just my friends."

"But, Mam, I thought..."

"What did you think, love?"

"Never mind, Mam."

When they were starting on the hard stuff about nine o'clock, Stan followed Beryl into the kitchen. She was just deciding to do a bit of washing up.

"Grand party, Beryl," he said. Sweat was gleaming on his high domed forehead and his eyes blazed from behind his thick lenses. "Beryl, I'd like to take you away for a weekend, like..."

Beryl was getting the idea that Stan was a fast worker. It seemed he'd been married three times and had left all his wives. When he wasn't wearing his cap, he looked less froggy and quite handsome in a certain way.

"Here," she said, shoving a tea-cloth at him, whilst she wiggled her fingers into her pink rubber gloves, and started immersing the plates in suddy water. You had to watch it with Stan. The devil found work for idle hands. She felt as thought a tidal wave was about to sweep over her. It might happen at any minute.

He was holding a plate in his big knuckly fingers and staring at her.

"Well, that's very nice of you, Stan... though you see I've got Big Striper."

"Who?"

"The cat - I can't leave him - I mean he was Billy's cat... Billy would never forgive me if..."

Just then she became aware of another presence in the kitchen. It was Eddie bearing a tray full of crockery spotted with chunks of pork pie, half-scoffed sausage rolls, dustings of powdered crisps and escaped pickled onions and toothpicks (cocktail sticks).

"Thought we'd best get shut of this lot," he said.

"Now that's very thoughtful of you, Eddie... oh, by the way, do you know Stan?"

"Er, yes," he said, "as a matter of fact him and me was in the same class at school - that's right, isn't it?"

Stan had turned round. His eyes had become frogspawn swimming in the ripples of his spectacle lenses.

"Is that right? Can't remember that."

"Oh well..." Beryl accelerated her washing up so that plates lay in glistening layers right across the draining board. The two men were staring at each other with threatening blankness in the way dogs or small children sometimes do. She was sure that ructions would follow.

"Do you think you could bring us another load in, Eddie, please?

Stan, buck up - we'll have 'em on the floor soon."

"Sorry, Beryl, sorry."

Eddie padded away with the tray flapping in his hand.

"We could have a fantastic time - just you and me."

"Like I said, Stan, it's very nice of you but I couldn't - not with my commitments."

"Come and give us a song, Mam!" Stu said, bounding into the kitchen. "Leave that lot!"

It was whilst Beryl was giving a rendition of 'Stand by Your Man' that she heard pots smashing. Her voice squeaked into silence and she muttered, "Just a minute!" and raced back into the kitchen.

Stan and Eddie were lunging at each other, both red in the face and breathing gustily. Strewn about the floor were shards of gleaming bubble-festooned plates.

"Bloody hell... what's going on here?"

"Sorry, sorry..." Stan's huge hands hung at his sides; Eddie's hair was sticking up. They both looked pink and guilty.

"I'll get it cleared up," Eddie muttered.

"We'll pay for the damage," Stan said, "really very sorry, Beryl... never meant..."

"No," she said, giving them a look which, although smiling, obviously meant 'drop dead!'.

They both became jumpy and placatory. Eddie fluttered about with the dust-pan and brush, and Stan stuck at the washing up. Nothing more was said.

At about midnight, when everybody was leaving, Beryl found herself alone for a few minutes with Eddie.

"Er, Beryl, I do hope you aren't mad with me, I wondered if you'd like to come round to Mam's for a meal next Saturday... I'm a good cook."

Thinking of that mouth-melting sponge Beryl said, "Thank you, Eddie, I don't think I'm doing anything just then..." (She knew damned well she wasn't.)

After Eddie had disappeared into the night, Stan still hung about. Beryl knew he was trying to get her by herself.

"I hope you're still speaking to me," he syruped. The syrup was deep and gooey.

She sensed Stan went in for big dramas and was only thoroughly enjoying himself when he had succeeded in stirring one up.

"Of course I am, Stan, why shouldn't I be?"

"Oh well... I just thought..." The dots in the frogspawn dilated and swam nearer. "You know, Beryl, love, I wouldn't offend you for the world."

"Good," she said.

"Well, what I was thinking - I could maybe give you a hand in the garden - you was saying the back was getting out of hand."

"That would be very nice, Stan."

"Okydoky... I'll get here next week, you just say."

When they'd all gone, Beryl looked round the place and gave a small sigh of satisfaction; not too much havoc had been wrought.

The following week saw Stan digging away in the back garden, wrenching out groundsel, twitch-grass and buttercups. Since Billy's death the garden had gone wild. Gardening was not the sort of thing Jason would have undertaken. It wouldn't have fitted in with his mohican and the earth would have spoilt his nails - he'd read something about Chinese emperors keeping their nails talon-length and that had become his own goal.

Beryl was very encouraging. "That looks real nice, Stan," she said at regular intervals when she called him in for mugs of white very sweet tea (he needed four heaped teaspoons). Beryl felt his high sugar consumption might be in part responsible for his hyperactivity.

He knew a lot of things, did Stan; could tell her all about welding and how to make a window-frame or plumb in a washing machine or a lav. He could also reel off which football team won when. What became apparent too was that he was madly impulsive. Before you could spit, he'd dedicated himself to something on which he focussed with terrifying zeal.

"Oh," he said, after a visit to her lav, "you need a new toilet, Beryl - there's a crack in the bowl - it'll spoil your floor. I could see to it for you."

"Could you really, Stan - well, I wouldn't say no."

"Say yes, then."

The Saturday rendez-vous with Eddie turned out to have distinct possibilities. Beryl, prinking her way through the lettuce frills and juicy prawn squiggles of the first course with her little finger extended, decided that Eddie had many assets.

When she'd reached the coq au vin and was spearing up button mushrooms and small cubes of ham and crisp parsley-speckled croutons from the rich brown juice, she was almost transported. The final delight were caramel-coloured eclairs from which the cream squooshed as she bit and the chocolate coating melted to give a bitter-sweet taste.

"It was grand, Eddie," she sighed, "a proper treat."

Eddie smiled modestly, "I used to go to cookery night-class, you know."

"It's loads better than you'd get in a restaurant."

Eddie glowed. His dust-grey hair became carved waves that shone pewter in the subdued wall-lights.

"Beryl," Eddie said, "er..." Here he began pleating the edge of the table-cloth. "Do you think..."

"Yes, Eddie?"

"Well, I was wondering if, well - I mean if you and me could, like, get married."

His usually stone-coloured face had become bright red.

"Oh, goodness me." Eddie, Beryl decided, was far more tricky to deal with than Stan. He appeared soft and feline, but there were his claws. You never knew when they might be unsheathed. He'd looked pretty warlike when he and Stan had laid into each other.

"I don't know what to say, Eddie... I mean it's not easy."

"How do you mean, Beryl?"

"Well, me being a widow and everything." She didn't think it would be tactful to refer to Jason at this point.

Somehow she managed to slide out of saying yes or no but she still thought Eddie looked crestfallen.

The following Monday morning a pink envelope dropped through her letter-box:

> Dear Beryl
> i am not very good at saying things and i am not a good writer either but i just want to tell you i would like us to get spliced i do hope you feel the same about me. You are the only one for me
> I will come round on tuesday
> Yrs. Stan

The writing was big and ungainly and he wrote I with a small letter and Beryl knew Mr Briggs at school had caned people for doing that, but it was her first love letter. She imagined Stan scouring the town for PINK paper. It stank violently of violets and bunches of what looked like pansies squatted in the four corners. She spent all morning pondering on the surprise of Stan's choice. Who would have thought that Stan Draper would have done such a thing? It was a gesture you might have expected of Eddie.

After her first surprise had passed, panic set in. What was she going to say to him when he turned up? She started thinking of a story she'd read once as a kid about a princess courted by many hundreds (or was it thousands?) of princes. There had conveniently been this great block of granite with a sword embedded in it. The prince who could heave the sword out of the stone would receive the hand of the princess in marriage. Well, Eddie certainly wouldn't come off too well in a sword-in-the-stone heaving contest - and poor old Stan was a bit decrepit for that. Now that would have been a problem, if nobody had been able to drag the sword out. Anyway, what if the princess had only fancied bits of the princes, and not one single person?

The more she thought about it, the more she realised that they were all survivors from the typhoon of life: they had been thrown up and beached. They belonged together, the three of them. Stan and Eddie were still effervescing with emotion. It reminded her of kayli fizzing when you'd licked your finger and stuck it in the bag of yellow particles. What they needed was guidance... a steady hand, and she could give that...

On Monday evening she rang them both up and invited them to tea the next day. She didn't let Stan get started about the contents of his letter because she said somebody was at the door and she had to go.

They turned up at 4.45; Stan first and then Eddie, both in their suits. Stan's would have fitted an all-in wrestler. It was double-breasted navy stripe, and had probably been a wedding suit at some time. Beryl wondered for which number it had been used. Eddie's suit was grey and too short in the leg. They both looked non-plussed at the sight of the other.

"Come on in," Beryl chirruped.

They bumbled in behind her and she led the way into the kitchen. She was giving them salmon and cucumber sandwiches and a bought fruit cake. "Not up to your standard I'm afraid, Eddie."

Neither of them seemed inclined to speak and that was unusual. They both sat opposite each other and Eddie kept clearing his throat. Stan hummed and played with his knife, tapping it on the formica. At last Beryl got the tea poured out.

"Come on, do help yourselves!"

There was a discreet munching punctuated by the clack of sliding dentures.

"Now," Beryl said - she felt she was about to give the opening speech at a meeting - "reason I asked you both here to tea is that I've had an idea."

They were looking at her - Stan's frogspawn eyes and Eddie's striped jungle-cat ones. She almost dried up with fright but forced herself on. No good caving in - that was what they were good at.

"Now all three of us are living on our own - think of what we're paying out in bills for lighting and heating, rent... if we all got together and lived in one house it'ud be a lot cheaper... and I mean, we aren't getting any younger, we could help each other - it'ud be better than a twilit home anyday, and that's what's in store."

They both looked amazed. Their eyes wobbled and stared.

"But..." Stan started.

"No buts," Beryl cautioned, grinning at him.

They didn't argue against it for long, and in no time at all Beryl was able to whip out the glasses and fill them with some poisonously sweet British sherry that she kept for festive occasions.

"Here's to us!" she toasted, and they all creaked up from the kitchen table, with Stan kicking the leg so that it almost overturned, and clinked glasses.

When the two men had left, Stu dropped in. Beryl was clearing away.

"Looks like you've had visitors, Mam?"

"Yes, love, my two new boyfriends, we're going to set up house together."

Stu looked dumbfounded. "But Mam, for goodness sake!"

"It's our twilit home," she said, smiling. She was imagining Stan pushing the lawn-mower down emerald stripes and planting herbaceous borders, whilst Eddie made jam tarts and swiss rolls and whipped up honey-gold sponges. And she? Well, she would be practising her Lotus position in the bedroom, or doing her flower-arranging and soft-toy making. She even had ideas for two new soft toys.

Messages

When the phone trills, I pick it up. "Hello," I say into the mouthpiece. "Hello." All I can hear is breathing - not what you'd call heavy breathing but a sort of listening. I listen too. "Hello," I say again. There's no answer, just the breathing, so I replace the receiver.

I sit quite still and look at the gas fire. It's years since all this happened before. Ken was on night-shift, just like he is tonight. The kids were asleep in bed. I was looking at something on tele, then the phone rang.

Hello, I said, hello. But there was only this weird breathing on the other end. I've heard about 'heavy breathers'; that's become a cliché. Some of the women at work used to say: Oh I've been getting a heavy breather ringing me up.

I wanted to ask them what these phone calls were like; how did they know what qualified as heavy breathing - was it gasping or that squeaky asthmatic rasping; or was it breathless panting, the sort you get if you're sprinting, or...? Anyway, of course I didn't ask.

After that first phone call I was puzzled - not shocked, just amazed and I sat for a while thinking about it. There were two more calls before I went to bed and I started staring at the phone. It had a life of its own and although it looked innocent, it wasn't. Before that I always liked hearing it ring, because it meant a change; something was going to happen; something new and I wanted excitement, romance...

The next day when Ken came home at seven and slipped into bed beside me, I was going to tell him, but I didn't. And then I was rattling the cornflakes bowls onto the table and slapping marg on bread for school packed lunches. After that, it was too late. I always meant to tell him, but somehow it didn't happen.

Now I didn't get the phone calls every night, it was just sometimes. A couple of nights might pass and then there'd be ring, ring and it was never when the children were up or when Ken happened to be in.

I began to feel there must be someone watching the house and when I went to work, I'd be glancing round. At that time we lived on an estate of new houses that they called 'Ghost Town'. I'm not sure why - maybe it's because they all look the same - brick semis with carriage lamps over the doors and a car-port and a scrolled metal gate, a hand-

kerchief lawn and border of roses. On a weekend the men'ud be washing their cars; there'd be the odd jogger prancing along in his blue
tracksuit, but it was basically very quiet.

I'd leave Ken in sleeping, and all the way to work I'd be wondering if he'd have any phone calls, and when I got back, I'd ask him how
he'd been - never: Has anybody rung? - and he'd say the gas meter chap
had woken him up or a double-glazing salesman or something... but
never a phone call.

On the nights when the phone didn't ring, I'd be on edge, feeling
that it ought to have rung. Who could be phoning like this? Was it just
some pervert who was working down the names in the phone book? Did
he find K.and J. Grayson and decide to phone us? But surely if he saw
K. and J. he'd know that it was a couple and if he wanted to prey on
somebody, this wouldn't help. What he needed was a single person.

The other possibility of course was a thief checking to see whether
someone was in - but then they wouldn't need to do that four times in
an evening - after the first call they'd know. It could be kids, but they
wouldn't prat about in the night, and anyway, why us?

When I was shopping at Tesco's nearby, I'd be pushing the trolley
down the aisles and watching to see if anybody happened to be following me. Any chap on his own, I'd feel might be the prowler. Whether it
was because of me staring or what, but then I'd find them frowning at
me, kind of savage and cheeky and I'd glare at my shopping trolley and
keep going.

There was a fortnight in June when it ceased. No phone calls at
all. I decided, it must have stopped for good; the snooper had got tired;
had switched victims. Snooper, victim. I suddenly started examining
these words. Was I a victim? I made a habit now of shutting the venet-
ian blinds in the kitchen as soon as it grew dark and I closed the lounge
curtains too - nobody could see in... and yet I felt they could.

A snooper must be a pervert; the sort of lonely type who preys on
women and then strangles them with their tights.

I had a good look at myself: I'm blonde and jolly - when I was
younger I reckon I was a Barbie doll type - now I'm like Barbie's mother. They say I'm a bossy-boots. Maybe I am, but that's me. I've always
liked stilettos and plenty of make-up and I'm not one of those who bags
about in slippers and dressing-gowns at home. I like a bit of style.

Well, I kept telling myself I was no victim: victims were pale,
twitchy lasses, not women like me.

I'd just breathed a sigh of relief and thought that's it, finished,
when the calls started again. Then they were regular, every evening.
Sometimes when the phone rang, I wouldn't speak, but if I didn't say
hello, there'd be more calls until I did.

I got so that I couldn't sleep at night for wondering if somebody was waiting outside. I'm not the sort who can go down and face an intruder. It's like mice. I can't bear mice but I couldn't kill one, I just have to run away.

The night I had four calls, I went round to see Elaine, my neighbour.

I've been getting these calls, I said, and I just can't stand anymore - somebody rings up and breathes...

Breathes, she said, breathes?

Yes, I said, never speaks.

Oh, you mean a heavy breather?

You could call it that.

She made me have a gin and tonic. She was an auxiliary nurse, a motherly woman - not a Jezebel. She mummied Lawrence, her husband. He was very tall and thin, a bit like a stick insect, and stooped and had these very dark eyes with glossy black eyelashes like spiders legs and folds in his cheeks.

I've decided I'm reporting it to British Telecom, I told her. They can intercept your calls.

Good idea, she said. Have you told Ken?

No, I said, I don't want to worry him... him being on nights.

So after I'd told British Telecom, I wasn't bothered with calls anymore. You would have thought I would have stopped worrying, but I didn't. I took to watching everybody I knew. What if it could be either of the neighbours - either Lawrence, or Frank on the other side? There was even the possibility of it being Ken. Now Ken is just a regular guy, but he has this jealous streak. If he as much as sees me talking to another man, he wants to know who said what, why. I've always considered jealousy proof of love - I mean, if he couldn't have cared less, it would have been a bit insulting.

I really didn't see how it could be Frank; he was only interested in football and pints... but then how can you say? I mean there can be all this craziness locked up in people.

Not long after the calls stopped, I was coming up the path and I saw Lawrence staring at me. He was supposedly trimming their privet. It was such a strange look, hot and cold at the same time. I didn't know whether I should speak or pretend I hadn't seen him. Anyway, I just looked across at him.

You can do mine next, I shouted, beaming like an idiot.

He kind of jumped and looked like I'd made an indecent suggestion, so I belted straight into our house and shut the door. I was blushing and I felt a bit shaken but I couldn't think why.

About this time I noticed that Frank, our other neighbour, always seemed to be grinning at me. He and his wife threw a Christmas party for the neighbours and he gave me a big hug and said:

Give us a kiss then, Joan, and before I knew what, I'm looking up his nostrils into all these hairs and his mouth's clamped on mine.

Well, of course, Ken didn't like that and it ended up with him thumping Frank and us going home and Ken being in a foul mood... and I started wondering again.

All this made me decide the breather must be either Frank or Ken... but I really couldn't believe it was Ken, my own husband. The thing about this, though, was that it made me ponder about whether you can ever know anybody. When Ken came home from his night shifts, I'd catch myself staring at his face and hands. Could this guy make creepy phone calls? Was there this other side to him, apart from the Dad who took the kids to the fair and the cinema and who'd buy me a red rose on Valentine's Day and take me out for a meal?

It began to get to me and one day about this time, I said to Ken:

We don't have to live here always, do we? Why don't we move somewhere else?

That's how we come to be living in this semi on the other side of the town. Since we've been here, all these years, the kids have grown up and now I've got a grand-bairn, and there's been no more of the phone calls - that is, not until tonight.

It's not that I've forgotten about them though - no way. They've always been at the back of my mind, because it's been like one of those unsolved mysteries and ever since, I've been uneasy. Then at times I've wondered if I've imagined it all, but of course I haven't - I mean, Elaine knew, British Telecom knew. I had the feeling for ages that it might have been Frank. Not now though. Frank, wherever he is, just lives for boozing - he's the sort of chap who just likes an excuse to touch women. Somebody of that ilk doesn't ring up and breathe in the phone or pinch knickers from washing-lines.

And Ken? Ken's the guy I've been married to all these years, my kids' Dad, and I've maybe done him an injustice by thinking he was the snooper and spying on him - to be quite truthful I've sometimes rung him up at work, just to see if he was really there.

Tonight, though, I've got the certainty... the proof... and even that makes me feel peculiar; because there are some unsolved mysteries that you get used to; they become just another piece of lumber in your life, like the fact that you can't stand mice.

This is how I know. Tonight I bought the evening paper. I always have a look down the death columns because there might be someone I know who's passed on. I was halfway down the Bs and I came to Brennan - Elaine, dearly loved wife of Lawrence, and I got a real shock.

Elaine was a nice motherly woman and I used to think it such a pity they never had any children. She always seemed a bit wistful underneath - she'd look at my kids with such longing.

When I'd thought about Elaine for a bit I decided I ought to phone Lawrence and say how sorry I was.

It got to ten o'clock and that's when the phone rang. At half past it rings again. My skin goes all cold and goose-pimply. I'm terrified. I pick up the receiver.

"Hello," I say, "hello." There's just the silence and the breathing and he's listening. I replace the receiver.

Suddenly I know what I'm going to do. I dial his number. The phone rings a couple of times and he picks it up. He doesn't say who it is.

"Lawrence," I say, and now I'm sweating, "Lawrence?"

"Yes," he mumbles.

"I'm real sorry about Elaine - I saw it in tonight's paper - I was just going to ring you, but you got in first."

"What?"

"You phoned me. I knew it was you."

"What?" he says again.

"Oh, don't play funnies - why do you do it?"

There's silence for a bit. I'm boiling.

"It's not me."

His voice sounds gruff and strange. I imagine his dark eyes and black hair which must be grey now, his sunken cheeks.

"Come on, Lawrence, come clean!" I find I'm kind of wheedling.

"I just wanted to hear your voice, sometimes I need to," he says.

All the wind whooshes out of me. I'm a collapsed balloon. I think of his big eyes that always look sad.

"Oh," I say, "oh, right..."

I'm not sure what to say after that because I feel I'm walking on a crust covering soft ground and it could crack open and then I'd be plunged into a quicksand, that would suck me under, just like that.

"I would never harm you."

"No, no, of course not."

Somehow I manage to say goodbye and the phone clicks off. I'm wishing now that I haven't unravelled the mystery because Lawrence, instead of being a vague figure in my memory, is swooping terrifyingly closer.

Beautiful People

It's the hen-night. Jayne has been invited by her Auntie Di to go with her to Luigi's, an out of town night club, for a Christmas knees-up.

Now Auntie Di, whom Jayne must not call Auntie but just Di, owns her own beauty-cum-hairdressing salon and when Jayne leaves school in a few months time, she's going to work there as an apprentice hairdresser. Up to now she's been a Saturday girl.

Di's salon is called 'Hi There' and it is painted white and has gold lamps decorating the front. Inside, the white and gold decor is repeated in white leather sofas and big gilt mirrors. A gilded rose spears a white specimen vase. Di is tall and has straight blond hair flicking her shoulders. A thin gold chain droops round her tanned left ankle. She never wears tights or stockings in the salon, even when there's snow on the ground outside. For work she's mostly poured into a white jump-suit which is open almost to the cleavage because, of course, Di is run off her feet.

There's never a minute to yourself here, Jaynie, she has told her niece. You have to watch your legs though - the veins...

'The Veins' are things to be avoided at all cost. Jayne imagines wobbly blue snakes humping up under the pale brown flesh and shudders... but Di hasn't got any, she's flawless.

In the salon two of the staff are male. They have thick pale necks, satin hair and soft voices and they wear white suits. Their fluttery fingers caressing the customers' hair as they cut or blow-wave it, mesmerise Jayne. There are three female staff. Steff is about Jayne's age.

Jayne is wedged in the back of the taxi between Steff and the older woman stylist. Compared to Steff, she feels gawky and fuddy-duddy. Steff's hair is blond and pinned up in a top-knot and a fringe trickles into her big blue eyes. Peach wings swoop above her eyelids. She's wearing a very tight, short black skirt, black stilettos and a little black top under a black jacket. In this rigout and with her dangly earrings, she looks thirty. Jayne is silent with envy.

"I like that big dark one best," Steff is saying.

"He's not got such a tight bum as the blond," Di says, "he kind of sags a bit."

"They're all gorgeous," the older stylist says.

"Who are?" Jayne asks, amazed.

"The strippers."

"Oh..." Jayne blushes as they laugh together. Their laughter somehow excludes her. She hasn't noticed that before because she's generally regarded as the pet.

Strippers! Only now does she realise that they are bound for a strip show. A wave of excitement hurtles her into the air. The older stylist, Gemma, has whipped out a spray and is directing it into her mouth.

"Can't be too sure," she says.

"No, you can't," Di says. She is gazing out of the window. She's always perfect; there's no need for her to worry about bad breath or B.O. or whether her bottom sticks out or her milk-bottle legs show. Jayne wants to be like Di; she's always admired her more than anybody else.

When they arrive at Luigi's, everybody joins the queue for the cloakroom. The air is gaspy with Poison, Chanel 19, Musk and hair-spray. Through a forest of little black dresses and fingers stencilling-in ruby lips and dabbing powder over noses and patting and pulling hair, Jayne peers at bits of her pale face. Her granny glasses gloom back at her. She looks ordinary. Very nice, Jaynie, her mother said, when she was leaving the house, very nice. That means, she's a mouse; a person nobody notices, a nonentity. Why is it she can never look as good as Steff? Only glossy people come to 'Hi There', which is a unisex salon. Steff knows how to chat them all up. She sticks her little finger out when she's cutting and keeps making eye contact with the faces in the mirror: Did you reelly... well I bet that was nice... well I never, aren't you clever... you don't say. And did he reelly... what a pity. Oh well, there's more pebbles on the beach.

She clops about in gold mules and you can see her knicker-line under her white jump-suit, and the men stare at it.

The audience in Luigi's on this evening are mostly women. They're all sitting at tables. The lights wink on and off over the bar and there's a message in gold and red: Happy Christmas.

They're having Christmas dinner and, whilst a female vocalist warbles "I'll always love you" into a mike, Jayne tries to push a chipola-ta sausage into her mouth without appearing to gannet it. What an ordeal to be eating in front of other people, but thank goodness there aren't any men watching!

Di and Steff and Gemma are having a discussion about men's bums and it weaves in and out of the singer's "I'll always lurve you..." Lurve gets lost in Di's clear, lazy voice. "I always go for a high, tight ass, can't stand men with droopy backsides..."

"Oh yer, look at him over there!" Steff indicates the retreating cocktail waiter, "it kind of spreads." Steff giggles. After wine, she's on vodka orange, and the light catches her scarlet lips and her earrings. Her flesh is plump and white against the silky black top. She's deadly sophisticated. She must know everything about sex.

"They'll be on any minute - they said ten o'clock."

"I'd like somebody like that lad in the Levis ad - that dark one - what a body - reel hard." Steff giggles into her drink. "I like 'em hard."

Di laughs too. The music pumps and swills and in the shifting light people's faces turn green and red and blue. The percussion vibrates the floor. Smoke jigs above the bar.

"They're on!" Steff squeaks.

And there they are, five men in policemen's uniforms. They sashay across the stage, smiling and wiggling their pelvises. The pounding of the beat deepens. They're easing off their tunics now and they form into a line and dance in formation. Their ties tease off. When their fingers are unbuttoning their shirts, the women begin to titter and shout:

"Come on, get 'em off, get 'em off!"

It's whilst she's letting herself peek at their torsos that Jayne realises that there is something very familiar about the man at the end of the line. It's Mr Thompson, Tommo, who teaches P.E. and English at her school, and looks like a Greek god. She feels her cheeks growing hot. It's embarrassing - she'd like to sink into the floor.

The men have smooth brown hairless chests and massive shoulders, their arms curve with muscle.

Wait till she tells Trace and Mand at school about Tommo. All the girls are in love with him. She's not sure what she's feeling - it's excitement but something else as well.

They prance about in their uniform trousers and Jayne stares at their braced shoulders, the planes of their chests and the pips of their nipples. Their flesh shines like oil. Their chests narrow to the shaft of their waists; their buttocks are compact pads of muscle under their trousers - she finds she's enjoying the way they move and the close fit of their trousers, the pillars of their throats.

When they come down off the stage and start dancing round the tables, fear makes her sweat. She looks across at Steff whose red mouth is wide with saucy laughter. The women are screeching. It's scary and funny and disgusting, Jayne thinks, and her mother would have a fit if she knew about it. Jayne just hopes Tommo won't come to their table. She glimpses the back of his head. The dark hair lies smooth and glistening against his skull and the way it grows in a peak amazes her. She's never been any good at games and P.E. and Tommo has put her in detention twice for being cheeky and not bringing her P.E. kit.

The men return to the stage and then slide out of their trousers. They're down to their boxer shorts now. One of them moves onto the centre of the stage and starts rubbing himself. 'Hammer' is going full belt. He's only wearing a silver G-string and as he runs his hands over his bulging thighs a great burst of green goo shoots out from the baggy hump between his legs. Everybody cracks out laughing and some girls are screaming.

"Show us then, show us!" the older women clamour.

The man is massaging himself with the bright green slime. Soon his entire body is gleaming.

Again the men circulate amongst the tables and all sorts of things are happening. The older women's voices are hot and rasping as they egg the men on to ever more daring forays. The girls are laughing with mounting hysteria, and the beat dongs and sizzles. Horror of horrors, Tommo is at their table, hanging over Di, who's shrieking to her back fillings with laughter. Jayne pretends all this isn't happening, but she can't help noticing Tommo's wedge-shaped thighs and his hands as they drag back Di's chair, and she's shocked that those fingers have written the word 'Composition' on the board and 'beginning, middle, end'. Di becomes someone else too. She's no longer that cool, beautiful blonde...

The throbbing of the music is deepening in insistence; the strippers and the older women are batting words to and fro and they grow ever wilder. Something awful is bound to happen. Jayne feels that they're teetering on the verge of it. And then it does. Three of the other strippers have climbed back onto the stage. They are gyrating, grinding their pelvises to and fro in a circular motion and calling to the audience to come up on stage and strip off. Nobody moves but the laughter gusts and the voices from the audience call, "Come on, ger up there, gerrup then!" At that Steff bangs up from her chair, she's giggling and clawing the air.

"Or right then - you just wait!"

She lurches between the tables, and Jayne, watching, wants to run and drag her back, but she daren't. Why doesn't Di stop her, or even Gemma, or the other older women? Jayne looks at their faces, but they're lost in the cheering like people at a football match. There's a steady handclapping now and the thunder of feet.

Steff is in the centre of the stage with the spotlights on her and she's grinning in a stupid, terrifying way... Her features are blurred and her eyes look mesmerised, as though she's not really there.

As the music thumps and quickens, she unbuttons her blouse; then she shimmys to and fro, throwing out her hips. The strippers are standing round her, clapping and grinning and making suggestive gestures. "Very nice, very nice... get 'em off!" a blond one wheedles.

With that Steff strips down to her bra. Jayne can hardly bear it; she wants to race onto the stage, cover Steff up, but she doesn't. It's so awful, she finds that her eyes have filled with tears. Steff's bra sails into the audience.

As the beat builds, everything flies faster and faster and the speed of the clapping increases until it snips the air. Jayne can't see for tears. She looks across at Di, hoping that her face will register something else, but she's grinning and clapping with the rest.

A great cheer bursts as Steff gets down to her black lace and nylon briefs. For a moment she stands there dazed and fumbling. The music and the screaming and cheering roll over Jayne in a great wave. Everybody seems to be caught in a spell and the roaring has a rapacity about it which chills Jayne. Then, just as Steff is about to peel off her briefs, Jayne finds herself getting up from her chair and rushing forward. She pushes past tables and up the steps to the stage. Her face is burning hot and her heart is pounding.

The strippers are wondering what she's about and they keep up the clapping, thinking maybe she's volunteering for a double act - but Jayne goes up to Steff. "Put this on!" she orders, as she urges Steff into her coat. Steff obeys. She's trembling and her face is sweaty and she has turned a cheesy white colour.

In the toilets Steff vomits and shivers; then she begins to cry, and Jayne makes her sit in there whilst she goes to retrieve Steff's clothes.

In the taxi on the way home Gemma says, "Been a good night out, hasn't it?"

"Yes, fantastic," Di says, smoothing her hair.

Jayne and Steff don't say anything and Jayne's thinking she'd better make an appointment to see the school's career adviser on Monday.

A Travelling Man

Lynne couldn't believe it when she saw him pushing through the swing doors. It was just like a dream, because sometimes in dreams he did appear to her, though with the passage of years even that didn't happen very often.

Maybe he wouldn't recognise her; maybe she was mistaken. She was drawing a pint of bitter for a regular and she kept her eyes down, concentrating on the head.

"There you go, love," she said, placing it on the bar. The customer handed her a five pound note. She knew he had come up to the bar and was watching her. Her heart was thumping as though she had been running. She felt dizzy and panicky. What was she going to say to him? Years and years ago she had imagined this scene, at first with dread and then with a sort of longing. She had never been clear why that should be... perhaps it was because she couldn't really shake free of him. He wasn't the kind of chap you could know or explain away.

For a second she thought Debbie or Ron would serve him, but no, he was waiting for her. There was no escape.

"Hello, love," he said. He had this deep gravelly voice. "Pint of bitter, please."

"Oh, hello." She kept her head down and stared at the beer hissing into the glass. He was still studying her. When she handed him the glass she found herself staring straight into his face. He was the same, only more battered - still with the cocky squaring of the shoulders, though instead of the long orange-gold sideburns now there were just white, finger-wide strips down the sides of his face and his hair had thinned and gone marigold-colour. His hazel eyes crinkled at her.

"How've you been, young woman?"

She wasn't a young woman anymore. A lot of years had shot by. She had to struggle to fasten the waistband on her trousers nowadays and if she got herself into the new white stretch pants, she had to leave her baggy blouse hanging out. She was heavier; she had seen things. She ought to know better than to be disturbed by him.

"Fine," she said, "fine." What the hell did you say after so many years? Years of what? How could you sum up days packing cod and haddock in 'Britfish'; toffee-making, watching the sweets hump along belts; a bit of shop work in a newsagents where she'd worn a daft orange uniform and a waitress cap and had her bum felt by the owner in his flash suit. And the men? Oh, there had been two or three who'd moved in for a time and then fluttered off or been thrown out by her. They'd wanted to be waited on, wanted a comfy number and no hassle. What had she wanted? She looked at him as he put the money in her hand. He was smiling, his lips lifting back from his teeth.

"Have one... it's been a long time?"

"Thank you, I'll have a glass of wine."

He'd taken up a position, leaning his elbow on the corner of the bar and was gazing at her under his eyelids.

"Cheers then, Lynne!"

"Cheers, Tex!"

"Been working here long?"

"A while. What about you?"

"Oh," he said, "I've just come back again - been working away."

She caught herself wanting to know where he'd been, what he'd done during all those years.

"It's just like that first time - remember, love?" His voice was thick with the past. She saw him swaggering in through the door at the 'Coach and Horses' with his denim shirt open down to the midriff and a mat of curly fox-red hair on his chest and the gold chain and the medallion swinging in it. His red-gold hair had waved back from his forehead and his conker-brown eyes had enchanted her with their winning light. The heels on his cowboy boots had sloped back. Straight up to the bar he'd strode and smiled at her - just as though there'd been nobody else present but the two of them.

He was John Wayne flinging the saloon doors open and shouldering his way to the bar, where she in a satin red dress with puffed sleeves and a décolletage and a gold heart-shaped locket hanging round her neck and her glossy black hair in ringlets was pouring bourbon into glasses for the cowboys.

"That'ud be telling," she said.

"You always were a shy girl."

"Was I?"

"Aye."

He'd come in every single evening after that first time and she'd got to wait for him. Sure as clockwork he'd be there, elbow resting on the bar. She heard about when he was a soldier stationed in Germany and how he could say: *Einmal helles Bier, bitte* and *Ich liebe dich* - all in that brown fudgy voice of his. It suggested passion, it was a crooning love-lilt. There was this other world that he knew too. He'd been to Aden and drunk tea with sheiks, swarthy men in white gear with white cloths wound round their heads. He'd seemed to be able to get on in these all-male worlds. It was what he knew. There was something brutally simple about it. Women talked about relationships; men were. She had never been able to fathom him because there were these great wedges of his life that she knew nothing about. She didn't know where he went or who he saw. He was employed in what he called the 'Construction Industry' - that meant he drove diggers, massive pieces of machinery that tore up the earth and gouged out holes in hillsides. Where he worked, men cursed all day long and sweated and talked sex and money and sandwiches. But he'd had this other side too - the sentimental. At least she'd thought it was that. He'd listen to Patsy Cline and Johnny Cash and look down into his glass. You felt he might howl with emotion, but at the same time his fists were ready to come up.

"Nice bar, this," he said, dead conversational, looking round.

"Yes, I've worked in worse. Gets a bit rough on a night sometimes though."

"Well, your bouncer looks big enough?"

"Looks can deceive."

"Aye, they can that... but you're a lovely girl, Lynne, and you don't change."

She blushed so that all her neck and chest went hot. He asked her about Steve.

"Oh, he's done very well for himself - works in a bank, got engaged last year."

"I wouldn't recognise him."

"No," she said, "you wouldn't." It hurt when she thought about that.

Steve was her only child, he'd been a little kid when she'd first met Tex. Steve's Dad had been caught up in a fight outside a pub and got knifed by chance, as you might say.

The vocalist and the two guitarists arrived and set up their equipment on a little stage.

"Evening, ladies and gentlemen. This evening we're going to take a wander down memory lane."

"Put your sweet lips a little closer to the phone, let's pretend that we're together all alone."

The voice yowled the words and they got lost in the ordering of pints and the conversation at the tables. Smoke twined about the faces of the men grouped round the bar and Lynne kept finding Tex looking in her direction.

In the breaks she asked him where he'd been.

"Oh, on the rigs a bit - don't mind the work and it's good money. Been in Saudi as well. Yer, it's hot there - me and this mate had quite a nice apartment though."

She listened to the descriptions of these mates and the parties and the secret boozy dos. It was all about six-packs and continuous drinking sessions that landed them comatose for weekends, and, in between, work and the sun and swimming pools and the shits.

The lines fanned about his eyes and the folds from nostrils to mouth corner deepened as he smiled.

Towards eleven he was looking at her with a sweet sad smile and his glance was so steady, she wanted to cry. All the old excitement leapt up in her. She was breathless and would find her eyes coming back to his. He magnetised her. It was something to do with his aloneness. She wanted to be his saviour and at the same time be saved by him.

He didn't smoke anymore, she noticed.

"Gave that up four years back," he said.

She didn't ask him why because she didn't want to know. If she heard his reason, she would start to see the cracks appearing in her great bronze cowboy who would crash open the saloon doors and rescue her.

There was, in the late night pub gloom with the singer's voice wailing and the cracks and creases hidden, a powerful magic. She was a young woman again, wanting and not knowing what she wanted, except that her husband, the boy next door, was dead and if he hadn't been killed he would have remained that nice guy, an easy sort. He'd been someone she knew through and through, and then he was dead, which had meant she had to start thinking... And then Tex.

"I've missed you - all through the years..." he said suddenly as she was standing for a moment, gazing over the tables away to the bright area where the vocalist was howling.

"Oh," she said.

"Did you ever think of me?"

She could hardly hear his voice and his eyes were hot and desperate. A wave of heat tingled up her from her belly.

"If you want to know, yes."

"I'd be out in Saudi... all that heat and sand and dust and no green thing and I'd think of you in the bar."

"Yes," she said.

"Two pints, a Bacardi and coke, a double brandy, love," a chap said, cutting off the moment.

"Yes, love," she said.

She began filling the pint glass and she remembered how she'd taken Tex home with her after that awful longing and those weeks of eye contact and molten limbs in the bar. Her denim-clad cowboy had come to live with her in the house on the estate with the metal clothes pole in the garden and the coal bunker - all those identical houses in rows and people all shouting about the same things and watching 'Coronation Street' and 'This Is Your Life' and 'Saturday Sport' and getting the frozen burgers and chips out of the deep freeze.

She'd given up the job in the pub because she'd thought she ought to be at home in the evenings with him and she'd got a cleaning job instead, but she needn't have bothered. Tex was never in. He'd appear for his tea at six and then vanish after complaining at the food.

Christ, not bloody chips again! Don't you know how to cook anything else?

Steve had had to keep out of his way and had spent a lot of time on the streets. She'd ended up night after night stuck before the tele with a sherry bottle at her elbow, having a solitary bevvy. He'd never shown before close on midnight, and when he'd sauntered in he'd have that haunted look she came to dread.

What's wrong, Tex? she'd ask. Is something the matter?

His face had twisted with the irritation of being asked and he'd often go and sit in the front room and play Patsy Cline and Jim Reeves over and over until the tears ran down his cheeks and then he'd climb into bed and fall asleep whilst she lay awake for hours tense and afraid. Something was wrong with him. She felt sure he'd got a woman somewhere, but she couldn't do anything about it. Her house was warm and comfortable and she thought she cooked nice meals and was always there to greet him - only none of it had been enough or somehow it had not been right.

The end had come when he'd complained again about the dinner, had strapped Steve for what he'd called 'being cheeky' and had come in at midnight with a face like stone.

You've got someone else, haven't you? she'd shrieked. I know you have... and you just use this place like a hotel... never in... just eat and sleep and complain.

His face had gone real white but she'd not been able to stop.

If you don't like living here, well go, just get out of my house!

He'd jumped straight up off the settee without a word and had banged upstairs. All his stuff had fitted into two flight bags because he travelled light. And he had left, just like that, disappeared into the night. His going had made very little difference to how the house had looked. It was only inside her that the marks had been made.

Ever since, she'd wondered where they'd gone wrong; where she had made a mistake; whether things could have been any other way. She had come to the conclusion that he must have had someone tucked away all the time.

She wondered, as the customer went away with his drinks and

she saw Tex still staring at her, whether he remembered how they had parted.

"There never was anybody but you," he said. He was confessing something that he wouldn't have done years ago.

Her cheeks burned, her heart blundered.

The voice was crooning another Jim Reeves number about wasted lives and lost loves. She noticed that the brush of hair showing through the open buttons of his denim shirt was now grey.

"Aye, lass," he said, "we're getting older."

The landlord called last drinks. It was late. She knew he was waiting to come back with her and that if he did he would lie beside her at night and eat his breakfast at her kitchen table but that she would never be closer to him than in that moment at the bar.

It brought the tears to her eyes as he was smiling at her. He could only love her as she stood behind the bar and he leant with his elbow on the counter and the tawny glass in front of him. He was John Wayne and as he drove his giant yellow machine or aimed his darts or talked in bars he was being how he had to be, how he wanted to be, because he had created his image. He couldn't be any different and he wouldn't compromise. And she? She must be that unattainable girl in the red dress, who smiled at him from behind the bar but never went home with him and cooked burgers and chips.

"Well," he said, as the pub began to empty and the landlord turned the pumps off, "well? Shall I escort you home, mi'lady?" He had such a sweetness in his face and the pouchy bits about his cheeks and jaw almost made her give in.

"It's late, Tex," she heard herself saying. He shrugged.

"Go on," he said. He was still smiling but she thought he looked hurt.

"Tomorrow night you can buy me a half in the bar," she said and grinned at him so that he wouldn't know that she had understood at last how he was; that she could never change his aloneness; that he needed his sadness and his longing and without them he wouldn't be able to exist. He was there in the Jim Reeves songs - that voice telling of the sweet sorrow at the heart of things between men and women.

"All right, little lady," he said in his low husky tone, and she watched his shoulders butting their way out. At the door he turned and gave a mock salute. She heard the old treacherous refrain in her head and saw the sadness in his face.

As she caught the last bus up to the estate, she thought of the consolations of a mug of cocoa and a plate of buttered toast and being able to sit in her dressing-gown with her feet propped up on the coffee table whilst she watched the late show on tele. She could set that against John Wayne and the red dress with the tight puffed sleeves and the boned bodice and the ringlets that had to be set in rags every night. At the same time she also realised that *she* didn't want him to be other than what he was. Settling her bulk into the sofa and stirring her cocoa she let herself dwell with pleasure and excitement on the idea of the next evening when she would see him push open the saloon doors and stride into the bar, his shoulders braced, his medallion swinging, his face tense with longing.

Stage Struck

I see this couple coming in. He's grey haired and big and he's wearing a black leather jacket and a polo-neck and he's got these kind of smouldering eyes that are cold as well. It's him I notice first as he's quite stunning - you have to look at people like that. Then I switch to her - she's in a black leather jacket and leather trousers, and she's obviously had a real expensive perm because her hair's all feathery curls. She's a lot younger than him. When I look into her face I realise it's Chrissy. She's always been lucky and I've envied her.

She doesn't see me at all because she's busy taking off her jacket and hanging it round the chair, then she's pulling down the cuffs of this frilly white blouse and settling it. Her little hands are fluttering about all the time.

They're discussing what to have. I move up to the table. It's then that she looks at me.

"Would you like to order?" I say

"Goodness, Sharon, hi! What are you doing in here?"

"Working." I can feel myself going red.

"Oh."

The bloke's looking restless.

"Aidan," she says, giving the guy a sweet, sweet smile. She's wearing lip-gloss over scarlet lipstick, and her mouth gleams. "This is Sharon Wells. I was at school with her and we were in the Theatre drama group together."

"Well, I never."

His voice is low and kind of clever, as though he's being sarcastic all the time.

"Sharon, this is Aidan St. James-Morrison, the film-maker."

"Hello," I mumble. "Are you just visiting then?"

"Yes... I wanted to see Mummy and Daddy - and Aidan said he'd drive me up."

"Now then, what about this sole? Is it fresh?"

"Oh, I should think so." I'm damned sure it isn't - even though this is a port, and used to be one of the biggest in the country, it guarantees nothing. It's all container stuff now... a man once told me fish goes to Leeds and then comes back.

"Mm... and the moules?"

Why the hell can't he say mussels? "Bound to be."

"Okay, we'll go ahead with those then... and get me the wine list, will you, Sweetie?"

He flashes me a white smile. His eyes squeeze into sapphire slits behind his heavy framed specs. His skin isn't lined much because it's very coarse and grainy and kind of knowy. You can imagine he knows all sorts. He's wearing some very exotic lotion too.

They've dumped their black leather hand-luggage near the table and I almost go flying over it. I'm wearing this little black dress and white apron and I feel a nerk.

This place has only been open a few weeks. It's meant to be the last word in restaurants and it's part of a shopping precinct that looks out onto what was a dock.

Some say millions have been spent on it - it's all glass, just like a gigantic conservatory, and it's packed with brand new shops. Everything's real expensive. How folks are going to buy any of the gear, I don't know, but nobody seems to worry about that. Loads are out of work, but they just keep on building new shopping complexes and cinemas.

I pass the order through to Sean, the chef, and he winks at me.

"That couple want a wine list," I say to the wine waiter. He lopes over. I see Aidan Whatsit interrogating him.

While I'm whisking piles of smudgy plates from tables, I keep peeking at them. I can't believe it's really Chrissy. She was always my best mate. I never thought I'd lose touch with *her*. We kind of admired each other: she's so dark and has a heart-shaped face, and I'm blond and have blue eyes. Right through school it was only her and me. We were the ones who got put into detention for lateness, smoking, being rude, not doing homework, having our skirts too short and too tight. Chrissy had to take a letter home after she'd said, So what! to the Head when she'd said, Christiana Elliot, your skirt is indecent.

And then we started going to the Rep - it was Chrissy who had the idea. I'd never been inside a theatre up to then - theatre was just a word, but folks like my Mam wouldn't ever have gone.

I'm going to be an actress, she said.

Of course her Mam and Dad working at university knew all about that kind of thing - she could get away with blue murder. She had a clothes allowance and her Nana would keep on slipping her tenners on top of that. We both wore total black all the time, and black nail varnish as well. Our arms rattled with silver bracelets. My ears were spiked right up the rims with studs and I went and had a butterfly tattooed on my shoulder, but that was later.

We joined the Theatre Youth Group, which meant I spent a lot of time selling ice creams at performances. She made it with the producer, of course. He had long black hair gelled back and in a pony-tail, and he wore little neck-ties and big boots and battle fatigues.

It was all that exciting I never wanted it to stop. We'd be down there four evenings a week, and we never got our homework done.

My Mam couldn't have cared less what I did. She'd split up with my Dad and was seeing someone else and I didn't like him.

"This wine's corked, man!" I suddenly hear Aidan barking at the wine waiter. "You'd better fetch me another bottle."

Chrissy's gone red, and she's staring out through the window at the water. She swings round and I catch her eye. She looks embarrassed.

Their mussels are ready. I hope she won't get poisoned. They look quite pretty, actually - all these navy-blue shells piled up in a heap and the white sauce steaming round them.

When I think how long we used to take getting ready before we'd go out - I'd make lists like: wash hair, press dress, put on make-up. My make-up'ud take three quarters of an hour and I'd never even visit the corner shop without it on.

I put the mussels down - a plate for each of them and the slabs of crusty bread he'd ordered.

He gives a long look at my legs. I feel his eyes travelling up me.

Chrissy smiles at me. "Thanks, Sharon," she says.

"Don't mention it." I smile at her. He ignores me and begins twining out the orange innards from the mussels and popping them into his mouth. He chews very vigorously, concentrating on it. Chrissy is picking about. I move away to a table with two businessmen.

"Now, dear," one of them says, "what's on today?"

I hand them the menues.

"Like to order?" I say. They're staring at me as well, like they've never seen a woman before - somehow it's bugging me today. Funny how you change. When I was fourteen, fifteen, sixteen, I loved it. I couldn't wait to grow up. Chrissy couldn't either. With our war-paint on and stillettos and little black dresses I bet we looked thirty in them days. It was all about sophistication and being clued-up. It's strange how when you're a teenager, you spend all your time trying to make folk think you know it all... and then suddenly you try to pretend you don't.

We were going to be international stars. I sold a lot of ice cream anyway, and I fell for Hamlet. Oh, God, did I love Hamlet!

He was one of these up-and-coming stars in repertory. I used to hang about when he was rehearsing. He was over six foot three - very

broad and blond and his hair waved straight back from his forehead.
When he gave me a lift on the back of his motorbike, it was like flying
to the moon. He had an old leather flying-jacket and he wore boots and
his hair would bounce forward. I could have cried every time I looked at
him because he was so beautiful...

I'm thinking of Hamlet as I write down the two guys' order for
soup of the day and Boeuf Stroganof.

They're obviously not going to let mad cow put 'em off - well,
they've maybe forgotten about it by now - most seem to have. Unless
tele's reminding 'em, and the 'Sun', they forget. It was the same with
the lamb and Chernobyl, and the salmonella and the eggs. There's
always something. I'm getting like my Mam.

Oh, Hamlet... I'd hear 'To be or not to be...' and shivers'ud be
going up my spine and my arms came out in goosepimples.

"Have you enjoyed them?" I ask the film-maker as I remove their
plates.

"They don't seem fresh to me - in fact, I've one here that positively
reeks. You shouldn't be serving this sort of stuff."

"Sorry about that, Sir."

My face is boiling and Chrissy's is red as well.

"I hope the sole's going to be better than this, if not I'll be regis-
tering a complaint."

There's a crumble of bread by his plate and he's scowling. It's like
some scene in a film. He seems to grow bigger and bigger. I look at his
hands lying on the table-cloth. Black hairs spider along their backs and
they're a dense, greyish white colour - fingers like the spatula things
the doctor holds your tongue down with so's he can look into your
throat. I shudder and start moving away with the plates. Hands can
tell you a lot...

When I return with the sole, he's looking out at the water in the
old dock - what's left of it. I'm feeling nervous. Chrissy croaks, "Thanks,
Sharon, that's fine."

I wonder what he'll blow up about this time. Chrissy's kind of
cowed. She never was like this before... Before. My God, what a lot has
changed since we were sixteen. I feel like I've been around a long time.

Seeing Chrissy makes me remember Hamlet so that I can almost
smell his body - I liked the sweaty sharpness of the orangy-blond hairs
in his arm-pits. Just looking at his naked back'ud bring the saliva into
my mouth. I wanted to eat him up.

Every night I cried when he died in the duel. Afterwards we'd
have a drink in the bar and he'd have purple shadows under his eyes
and look a bit old - he was eight years older than me, anyway...

That time was magic - we were suffering and crazy and couldn't get enough of everything - nobody else seemed to exist. It was always evening and we were always waiting for the hush before the curtain goes up. I think of big sheets of mirror splodged with brown and Hamlet's pale clever fingers applying sticks of grease-paint to his cheeks, concentrating and staring into the mirror: everything was charmed and kind of on the edge. The Rep had these discos in the theatre at the end of every season, and the music'ud be howling and I was on a high all the time... I think I was so high, I didn't understand what it all meant when it happened...

They've finished the sole. He's left a lot of his.

I hear her say, "Aidan, it doesn't really matter, does it?"

"That's where you're wrong."

"You won't ever let anything drop."

"Why should I?"

I don't dare ask if they've enjoyed it.

"Would you like a sweet?"

"No, just coffee?"

"Yes."

They don't seem to be saying anything. He's staring straight ahead of him and she's messing with her spoon, stirring the coffee.

I can see the tall masts of yachts on the Marina - millionaires' playground. It's weird to think of all these smart places stuck right in the middle of the boarded-up shops and run-down areas where there isn't anything anymore.

He's signalling me. I go over.

"I want to see the manager."

"Oh, yes." I'm blushing again.

"Kindly tell him that I wish to make a formal complaint."

I'm just hoping Andy's around. He is, and I tell him.

"Like that, is it - fetch him into my office."

I go back.

"Would you like to come this way, please?"

While the film-maker's in with Andy, complaining, I go back to Chrissy.

"Oh, Sharon, I'm sorry," she says. "He's not easy... nearly drives me mad."

Tears are shining in her eyes. "He's got a list - a list as long as your arm - and he never forgets anything... and it can all come up again at any time."

I don't know what to say.

"Come into the ladies," I mutter, because I know other tables are earwigging.

"How're you?" she asks. She's staring at her face in the powder-

room mirror and getting her compact out and starting to dab at it.
She'll have to cover up the snail tracks down her bronze cheeks.

"Okay."

"What happened with...? I thought you'd have been..."

"I lost it... ectopic pregnancy."

"Well, that must have been a relief."

"No," I say, "I was devastated."

She looks at me in amazement and then becomes embarrassed.
When she got pregnant by the producer, it was just a matter of a private clinic and Mummy and Daddy paying up. She thought with me
and Hamlet it would have been the same... but it wasn't.

"Have you finished at Drama School, then?"

"Yes - that's where Aidan spotted me... Oh God, I wish he hadn't."
She's fluffing blusher under her cheekbones and using a fine brush to
paint in her lips. "I look ninety," she says, standing back and gulping.

"Twenty-one," I say, "it's prehistoric."

"Do you know, I thought it was going to be quite different... didn't
you?"

"Yes," I say. I'm thinking of that summer, wandering about in the
hot streets in my black leggings and baggy T-shirt and with split plim-
solls on my feet, feeling the baby inside me. I was swelling up but I
wanted to be a lot bigger, I was so proud. I'd be glancing into all the
prams at the babies in sun-bonnets who were sitting up and chortling
at flies and leaves, the way they do - finding everything fascinating.

"I hadn't wanted it at first, you know, but then I was glad... I
couldn't wait. It was the happiest time of my life." I find I can tell her
straight, like I used to be able to.

She's still staring at her face, but I know she's only doing that so
it won't put me off and embarrass her.

"My breasts had gone real big... all of me... Hamlet was kind of
pleased, once he'd got over the first shock - he said he'd marry me... but
I wasn't bothered about that. I just wanted to be near him."

She turns round then and sort of sees something in my face
because she puts her arms round me and we both bellow on each
other's shoulders.

It's like we're crying for that time when we were sixteen and it
was all going to happen, and now we're twenty-one and it's not like we
thought, and we've lost something...

"Oh hell!" she says suddenly and drags herself away. "He'll be
furious. See you, Sharon ... I'll write..." And she rushes off.

A customer comes into the powder-room and I take a deep breath
and go back into the restaurant. There's no sign of them, they've gone.
Andy is staring about. His face is turkey-wattle red.

"There's some nasty bastards about," he snorts.

When I knock off, instead of walking straight home I go along the old dock-side - the bit that's left - and down onto the Marina. The yachts are creaking a bit in the wind off the estuary and jigging up and down on the black water. I look over at the old warehouse they've converted into a posh hotel. It was all different when I was a kid - it was just a warehouse then that a guy painted and I noticed the picture in the art-gallery when we went round with school, and that's when I really saw it for the first time.

Hamlet showed me a lot of things too - he had this low, smooth voice, and when his mouth formed the words, I could see them - they weren't flat anymore on a page.

I go on walking and I come to the place where the ferry used to sail across to Lincolnshire. The water slaps on concrete and wooden bollards. It's a dark, writhing stretch and I can see some tall chimneys over at Barton or somewhere.

Hamlet moved to London, just after I lost the baby. It was going to be the bright lights - Royal Vic or whatever - but when I wrote him, the letters came back unopened, and it's like he's dropped into a pit. Silence.

It's funny how all these warehouses and docklands have been made over into something else kind of modern and a bit flash but inside 'em there's traces of what they were before - just a feeling, as though ghosts are around. Me and Chrissy are like that - we're going on, we've slapped on our blusher and we're pretty with-it, but there's the wreck underneath - what's left from her producer and my Hamlet... the ghosts of babies. Only everything seems to change into something else after a time, and maybe that's not such a bad thing.

I turn back now and start to trek home and it's then that I find I've been crying because my face is all wet. Now I can't wait to get home and have a mug of tea and a fag. I feel very tired, as though I've just been through something...

The Swimsuit

When Syd Burns handed his wife, Tanya, her birthday present, he asked her if she would come to the bedroom with him.

"I want to see you open it in there."

"All right, love." Tanya felt the oblong parcel. It crackled and its silver paper spotted with fat scarlet hearts dazzled her. "I'm that excited!"

"Come on then!"

Once in the bedroom, Tanya peeled back the sellotape with care whilst Syd waited, racing his fingers along the dressing-table top. Usually Tanya said: No racing at Sandown, when he did that. Today she was too excited to notice. It was her big five 0. The kids were due round later with their contributions. Dum, dum Syd's fingers went. He would have had the paper off in a jiff. He'd spent ages choosing the present.

"Bloody hell," Tanya said, "eh, look at that!"

The foil fell away to expose the picture of a dark-haired girl wearing a silver swim-suit. Its cut-away legs revealed brown thighs with the glittering crotch nestling between them. The girl had one hand on her hip and her pelvis jutted forward, a swatch of brown hair sprayed her left shoulder. Her feet were posed in high-heeled, strappy sandals. She was smiling at the onlooker.

"Go on then, get it out, Tan!"

"Goodness me!"

Tanya eased out the silver garment. It felt like very smooth emery paper and yet was seductively soft. The touch of it alarmed and excited her.

"Well, what do you think?"

Syd always asked her that question. They'd spent twenty-five comfortable years together and were looked upon by friends and neighbours as the ideal couple. They took mutual decisions and didn't argue much. Syd was a family man and adored their three kids. Tanya's nets gleamed, her paintwork glittered and her Yorkshire puddings were as light as puffballs.

"Oh, goodness me!" Tanya was still staring at the swim-suit which she had placed on the bed.

"Put it on then, Tan!"

"I don't know about them legs!"

"Go on, give it a go!"

"I'll put it on in the bathroom - give you a surprise like."

"Okay, but put a sock in it then, lass - we'll have the kids here next."

In the bathroom amongst the avocado suite and gold-plated taps that Syd had magaged to plumb in himself with much cursing and heavy breathing, Tanya wriggled out of her candy-pink leisure suit, white bra and pants. She started to insert her legs into the swim-suit. What a number! The cut-away bits revealed ripples of pinkish, piggy-looking flab and tufts of pubic hair that reminded Tanya of couch-grass on a balding hillock. Bits of her squirmed out of the silver skin and would not be contained. She stood with her back to the mirror and tried to squinny at her bottom. Two large creased suety blobs squeezed the seat of her swim-suit into a silver string which disappeared into the crack between them.

"Bugger me!" she said.

Meanwhile in the bedroom Syd stopped racing the horses at Sandown and lit a cig. He sat down on the bed and let his thoughts run on a little frolic. The room was hot with late afternoon sunlight - perfect. Then his gaze strayed back to the girl on the packet. She was looking straight at him. Her cheeks had the golden-pinkness of a ripe peach. All of her looked succulent. He wanted to leave a love-bite on her neck, like he used to on Tanya's when they were courting. The girl's smile was very sweet - sweet and sincere and sexy, all at the same time. The silver suit must have been painted on her. It emphasised the lovely swell of her breasts and made her legs look as though they reached up practically to her collar bone. What a girl!

Suddenly Tanya's mop head of grey permed hair and her pink NHS specs shot round the door.

"I don't know about this, Syd," she said.

"Come on in and show us then, love!"

"Well..."

"Oh, come on!"

His eyes encountered her bosom which bolstered around her waist and oozed out at the armpits. They swam over the jellying of her thighs and here and there the mad blue squiggles of veining. He took a long drag on his cig.

"Yes, er, yes..."

"I couldn't wear this out, love..."

"No, nor you could." His tone was flat.

"I'll have to take it back, love... sorry about that."

"Don't bother - I'll give you the cash - just give it here... I'll see to it."

Tanya was surprised but she didn't argue with him. What could he do with a swim-suit like that? Syd restored the garment to its packet, looked at the smiling siren and lumbered off downstairs, leaving Tanya staring at herself in the bedroom mirror. She saw this tall slim girl standing by her side; this kid who caused her own hips to look like sugar-pot handles and her face an ordnance survey map by comparison. The lass still drifted around. She unsettled the day and made Tanya's new tricel trouser suit all wrong. When had this wattly jaw and the blocks of flab stolen up on her? They had appeared without her ever having noticed, because she was always so busy. The day grew spiky. She wished they hadn't planned the family party.

The kids gusted in, hugging her and filling her arms with parcels. She noticed how Syd didn't say much and confined himself to deep glugs at his whisky glass. She kept her fingers away from the three pound Cadbury's milk chocolate assortment box which someone had brought.

After the day of the big five 0 everything began to change. For one thing Syd bought himself a new black leather bomber jacket, a pair of black jeans and some cotton polo necks. But most amazing of all, he returned one Saturday afternoon with a gold sleeper in his left ear.

When their sons brought their live-in girlfriends to the house, Syd chatted them up and gave them long cuddles as they were leaving.

"Me Dad's shakin' a leg!" Darran, their eldest son remarked when he noticed Syd's earring. "You want to watch him, Mam." They all laughed.

Tanya smiled grimly; she saw again the silver girl on the swim-suit packet.

Syd saw the silver girl too. He'd be high up on his ladder under-coating window-frames when he might glance down and spot the girls going by: girls with long dark hair blowing in the wind and skin-tight sweaters, thick belts pulling in tiny waists and blue jeans to show off their endless legs. They rocked on platform heels and opened their scarlet lips to screech with laughter and they lolled against each other over a private joke. He saw their flawless peachy skin and he couldn't stop staring. Which of them would fit into that silver swim-suit? At times he came within an inch of plummeting to earth, so transfixed was he by the sight of them.

He took to having pints in city centre pubs where he hoped to catch sight of the silver girl again. Sometimes she was perched on a bar stool and he would be presented with her sweet young profile and her upward-tilted breasts. Her red lips gleamed, her white teeth flashed as she smiled.

On leaving at eleven o'clock he'd glimpse flocks of exquisite crea-
tures all hovering about the entrance of LA's, the central night-spot. He
fixed on white blouses, long shiny legs and wiggling bottoms, and his
nostrils twitched with the aura of scent and the whiffs of under-arm
deodorant and hair-gel. Oh, what intoxication!

Once home, he'd go to his garden hut where he kept his tools, his
lawn-mower, any spare paint tins and his decorator's equipment. There
he opened the second drawer of his steel cabinet and lifted out the
packet. The silver girl smiled at him. He took out the swim-suit and let
his hands roam over it. She stood before him, his silver girl, flicking her
thick dark hair over her shoulder. Then Tanya called, "Cooee!" It was
time for cocoa and sandwiches. He didn't want cocoa and sandwiches;
he wanted to be at LA's leaply wildly to the twanging electric guitars,
whirling his silver girl round and round and feeling her hot breath on
his neck.

"Do we always have to have this?" he snarled at Tanya. She shot
him a dense look, which he couldn't be bothered to interpret, and didn't
answer.

Shortly after that he stomped off to bed.

. . . . .

Tanya's life too had not remained untouched by the silver girl.

"I feel as though I'm just about ready for me twilit home and me
bath-chair," she confided in her neighbour, Babs, after the fateful five 0
day.

"Why don't we get off to that step-aerobics and then have a
sauna?" Babs suggested.

Before she knew what, Tanya was on the back row of the lines of
ladies in leotards, plopping up and down on her step. She thought her
hamstrings would snap but she persisted. Then came the luxury of sitting on benches in the swirling steam, turning a shade of lobster and
thinking of the handfuls of flab which must surely be melting away.
Step-aerobics three times a week, sauna, swimming; no more chockie
bickies with mugs of chocolate. She was measuring herself against the
silver girl.

Next she went blond, a dizzy white blond, and she bought some
gold hoop earrings. She gave herself long appraisals in the wardrobe
mirror. Sure, she was no teeny-bopper, but she observed that a certain
raddled charm was emerging. It created its own intoxication. She began
enjoying zizzying her arms about and plopping up and down off the step
and watching the teacher prancing back and forth. The music and the
voice set up a mesmeric pattern.

One day on the back row with her, she noticed a chap who looked as though he'd had a tractor driven over his face. His diamond eyes squinted and his voice grated. It had a deep gravelly honk.

"Hiya, lass, you've got a good leg on yer," he said when they were coming to the end of the session and were standing steaming at the back of the hall.

"Is that right?" she said, giving him her red-lipped beam.

"Yer, you have an' all... going in the sauna, are you?"

"Yes," she said, "me and Babs."

"Join you then."

So they sat in the steam on the wooden benches and the man yarned.

"Oh, yer, there was this maharaja - he had a diamond as big as an egg on his turban..."

"Is that right?"

"Don't you believe it then, Tanya?"

"Course I do, Sam." They were on first name terms by now.

Sam's tales made her forget to vacuum the stairs and clean down the paintwork. She didn't bother to make Yorkshire puddings either, there was no time. She even forgot about the ham for the eleven-fifteen cocoa and sandwiches routine - anyway, she'd given up on that, it was flab-inducing. Now there were days of tropical heat in the step-aerobics emporium and the sauna and swimming pool. Limbs in shiny body-stockings flashed; music pounded; the beat juddered and thumped like a mighty heart; sweat blistered faces. In the sauna the heat intensified. It was all heat and moisture and slipperiness and tales of white temples and people being beheaded and snow gleaming on jagged fangs and dead bodies being pecked to white bone by vultures.

On a Friday morning Syd, up his ladder painting away but always on the alert for the girl who would fit the silver suit, happened to glance down. There, below him, were two people who shocked him for some reason. He must look again. What was it that arrested his wandering thoughts? They were laughing together, laughing uproariously and they had a curious vividness about them that made them stand out from all the other passers-by. The woman's candy-floss hair shimmied in the breeze; the man had a craggy shape like some all-in wrestler. They both had faces you wouldn't forget... and yes... yes, it was Tanya.

His heart gave a great dong and he almost tumbled from his ladder. He wanted to shout, but he stopped himself just in time. For the rest of the day as his brush worked, slapping on paint, and smoothing, he fought the urge to rush home. He was angry. His head ached, his hand shook so that he kept having to wipe up splatters of paint. What the hell was this?

When he was finally at home, washing himself in the avocado

bathroom, he didn't know how he was going to broach the matter. He wanted to look at Tanya properly... he somehow felt he hadn't got a hold on life anymore. Even the bathroom taps looked dull and there were soapy splatters on the window. Something had been happening whilst he hadn't been watching. It alarmed him. He decided not to go to the pub - better stay in.

Tanya put his microwaved dinner before him.

"Where's yours?" he said.

"I'm not having any, love."

"Why not?" he was staring at her now. Her hair was different - earrings, lipstick... she was somebody else. It bothered him.

"I've had mine earlier on."

"Oh."

"Aren't you off out, then?"

"No."

"Right, well, I've to go out - thought as you'd be out anyway."

He heard her moving about upstairs and then she shouted, "See you, love!" and he heard the gate click. Gone. He picked at his Bird's Eye dinner for one. Later he sat before the tele, not really seeing anything, just staring at the jittering figures. Finally he blundered out to the hut. For some time he messed about putting his paint tins straight, aligning his jars of nails and his colour charts. Then his eye fell on the shears he used for trimming the privet hedge. He had sharpened them recently and they had grey gleaming blades. He wrenched the second drawer open in the filing cabinet and hauled out the silver girl, then he hacked her to pieces. Scissoring the blades across her neck, her pert mouth, until the hut floor was covered with fragments of silver cloth and paper.

The kitchen light flicked on. She was back. He waited for her to call Cooee, but she didn't.

The Great Divide

When certain things happen, it's as though they're predestined. And that's how it was on that Saturday afternoon in November. I'd been shopping all morning, looking for an outfit. My Mum could just as easily have been with me, and if she had been, I dare say it wouldn't have happened. On that particular Saturday she'd arranged with my Dad to see my Auntie Alison in Leeds, so I was on my own.

I'd tried on loads of these little suits - the sort of thing I might wear for work. In a solicitor's office you have to look smart - though of course I didn't want it for work. Somehow none of them seemed right. I'm blond and the red made me look anaemic. Perhaps black... but you wouldn't wear black for this occasion. My back was aching with so much leg-work. I'd been belting all over town. That was when I decided to go into this big old place that used to be some sort of Reading Room, only now it's been revamped into a pub and they serve meals and coffees and sandwiches. Oddly enough I'd never been in there before and I was a bit nervous, but I liked the atmosphere. It made me think of hot foreign places because there are big metal ceiling fans and brocade wallpaper and everything's scarlet and gold.

I ordered a pizza and bought a coffee and then I went to sit at one of the tables where there was a bench seat so I could lean back and look at other people.

A girl brought my pizza and I'd just started to eat when I saw him come in. He went to the bar to place his order and then he half turned and was looking straight at me. My heart was blundering about like mad. He hesitated and starting mounting some little steps up to the level where I was sitting. It was terrifying. I didn't know what to do.

"Hi, Caroline," he said, "mind if I join you?"

"Feel free!"

He took the chair opposite me so I had to look at him.

Rajiv is about six foot two, very slim and his thick, straight black hair is combed back from his forehead and he has it fairly long. His chestnut brown eyes gleam behind his metal-rimmed glasses. All his movements are easy and fluid. They mesmerise. As I watched him I remembered all sorts of things. For instance, he takes size ten shoes and there are places on his body where his colour changes. His elbows are browner than the palms of his hands or his chest or the soles of his feet, and his skin is as smooth as oil.

You can tell that he comes from somewhere exotic just by the way he moves or the sound of his voice. Even though he's lived all his life here and has an accent like mine, the quality of his voice is different.

"What are you doing here?" I asked.

"Lunch hour. And you?"

"Shopping - trying to get an outfit. You working for your Dad then now?"

"Yes - I'm doing most of the managing."

There were masses of things I wanted to ask, but I was scared. His parents have three shops that sell jeans and sweat shirts, all sorts of casual gear, as well as cotton blouses and skirts and velvet jackets and silver jewellery and dangly beads from India. In the shop with Indian imports it smells of sandalwood and spicy things. Everything's musky. I used to love shopping there but I couldn't visit it anymore. I might have run into one of the family - maybe his Dad - and that's the last thing I've ever wanted to do. His Dad is short and dark brown and has a face like a falcon and I used to feel he looked through me to the other side. It was as though I didn't exist at all. He refused to admit I was there. Rajiv's Mum would be hovering about in her saree and her eyes were like brown glass. She wouldn't look at me either.

I didn't want to remember that because it hurt and it stirred up bitterness I thought I'd forgotten. I just wanted to be able to talk to him in an easy way and maybe I'd tell him my big news.

"Do you ever see anybody from school, then?"

"Sometimes they come in the shop."

He mentioned a couple of kids who were in our class. I could hardly believe that we'd spent all those years together at school, first at primary and junior and then in sixth form college.

"What are you doing now then, Caroline?"

"I'm a private secretary for a solicitor."

Silence again. I decided he looked somehow like his Dad. He'd got the same big curved nose and he seemed very serious. Earlier on he used to laugh a lot. His face had set into grown-up, haughty lines. It pained me to see that as well. I could imagine him all day long in that shop with the wailing music and the musky scent and those floaty dresses and flowery blouses with the draw-string necks and gold bits and the pictures of gods and goddesses - Shiva and the Elephant god in gold and bright red and blue.

"Very nice."

"How's your family?"

"All right, thank you."

He was looking into my face and you would never have known that anything was happening except for this little pulse in his cheek - something just flickered and his eyes were those of a hawk, gold and dreadful, and I could feel them boring into my forehead.

"I saw you once in town with your wife."

Yes, and I couldn't forget it. She was wearing a saree with a coat over it and her thick black glossy hair hung in a plait down her back and she was pushing a baby-buggy. The sight of them had made my heart bang and my skin freeze and I'd rushed into M & S although I'd been desperate to see her and the baby and know where they were going. But I was afraid that he might turn round and see me. That would have been unbearable.

Another silence. I didn't think I knew this person - he wasn't young anymore; he didn't joke. They'd got him tight and they'd never let him slip away. We were twenty-four but he might have been forty-four from the look of him.

"Did you?" He smiled then, an awful, sad smile.

"You'd got the baby with you."

"We've two kids now."

"Oh, that's nice."

I felt I hated him and I wanted to make him pay. I wanted to slice through all that politeness and find what was underneath.

"Actually," I said, "I've got some exciting news."

"Oh yes?" He was giving me his very polite smile now, the one he'd use if we'd had a row.

"I'm getting married next week."

"Very nice." The smile was still there only it made his face look sterner than before. "Do I know him?"

"Warren Shaw - he was in our class." Of course he knew Warren - they'd been best mates once.

"What's he doing now?"

"He's in computers."

What was there to say after that? We carried on drinking our coffee and by this time I'd finished my pizza, though I hadn't enjoyed it.

"Give Warren my best wishes," Rajiv said after there'd been silence for ages. It sounded weirdly formal when I thought of the way we'd been at school.

There'd be those times after school, walking home. Warren and Raj would be wheeling their bikes and going on about some stroke they'd pulled on Mr Grayson, the chemistry teacher. We wanted to be by ourselves, Rajiv and me, but Warren always seemed to be tagging along. They'd both be at my gate and I had to keep my eyes anywhere but on Raj - though I just wanted to stare at him. He made me dream of foreign places; of the Taj Mahal, that great white building you see on travel posters; dark men in narrow high-necked shirts and white trousers and women in sarees. There'd be incense winding up and white cows lumbering by and elephants and Maharajas in satins and jewelled turbans like I'd seen in films on tele, and I thought how marvellous it must be - not a bit like the houses on our estate, all boring and the same. But when I used to ask Raj about India, he'd just laugh because he'd never been and it seemed to embarrass him to talk of it. I could never understand why.

It's no good asking me, he'd say, and shrug. I don't know any more about it than you...

I thought he'd never ask me out. We always seemed to be looking at each other but pretending we weren't. I'd be unable to concentrate on anything because I was thinking of him and he'd be sitting at a desk on the other side of the room. I might run into him at break-time in the canteen but I'd not look at him. I didn't want him to know I fancied him like mad, so much so that I dreamed of him at night. That was another peculiar thing - I'd think we'd done things together; that we really knew each other, but it hadn't happened. It was only in my dream.

Each evening after school we'd be standing outside my gate and I'd be waiting for him to say something and he wouldn't.

Whilst we were in the pub that day, sitting across from each other, it was just like it had been outside my house and me in my black leggings and striped T-shirt lolling on the metal gate and him, the dark prince, leaning against his bike and eyeing me up.

All the time this secret thing was between us and we seemed to be holding our breath, waiting. How did it happen like that? I don't know. For a long time he was just Raj, a brown kid in our class, who had to suffer a lot of aggro from some lads and who kept himself apart - not that anyone would notice unless you were looking. And then suddenly we were stealing glances at each other and it was all sparking and flaring.

When we used to be outside my house talking about other kids at school or something we'd seen on tele, I'd be tensed up, waiting for him to say he'd best be getting on home. Now I was expecting him to leave at any minute and I kept up this inane chatter about Dawson & Sons where I work and how Warren and me were going to live in a rented flat for the time being because of mortgages being difficult and building society repossessions making us nervous. He just went on nodding and smiling. Then I asked him about his shops and the recession and were they managing.

"Oh we're scraping along," he said, "anyway even if we wanted to sell up, we couldn't now - the property market's stagnant."

He was bound to rush off soon and then maybe I'd never see him again for years on end unless I called into the shops and then he'd be lounging there near the cash desk like his Dad did. He'd draw farther and farther away from me into that foreign little circle he lived in...

"I sometimes miss school, do you?"

"Oh yes," he said, "yes, I do."

"I can hardly believe in those times."

That wasn't true because I could, only too easily. I knew that whatever was happening between us was like a raging fire in a tinder-dry building; it could consume us.

There was the cricket match. He was always in the team. The afternoon sizzled and I sat drinking coke and watching him bat. The match went on quite late and when it was over, he loped up in his white flannels and open-necked white shirt. I saw his long brown throat and the sweat gleaming on his forehead and I thought of all those billions of brown men in white tunics and trousers and women with long blue-black hair, and the sun blazing. There'd be mosques and Hindu temples and people plunging into the Ganges. I had this dream and we were right in the middle of it.

That was the first time he ever kissed me. It was round the back of the changing rooms. We kind of bumped up against each other and I was shaking. When I saw his brownness up close it seemed strange to me - he was a part of something else. But then again he'd been born in the same town as me, maybe in the same maternity hospital, so he couldn't be diffferent. This feeling of being apart but linked unbalanced me.

He walked me home after that and I was floating, and everything about me - the lines of brick terraces and the newsagents and the sports shop and the supermarket - all were changed. I wanted to dance about and leap in the air. He held my hand but only until we came to my street and then he let it go.

"Are you happy?"

I couldn't believe he was asking me such a question. Was I happy? I didn't think about it. I was marrying Warren because he wanted us to and I've always been very fond of him...

His question hung in the air and got lost in the Heavy Metal booming out from the juke-box. "I don't know," I said, "what about you?"

"It's not something I dare to think about."

And he shot me a glance that made my skin freeze. I was the one wanting to draw back now. There were things I'd always felt I'd say to him if we ever met again. I just looked down at my hands.

"Shall we get out of here?"

I nodded. Where was there to go anyway?

His car was parked round the corner and he drove us down to the pier. I was glad he'd chosen there because it's wild and it's always made me think of journeys to far-off tropical places.

It was deserted and the wind off the estuary was belting in our faces and the brown waves slapped under the planking as we walked out.

There was something really terrifying about this because what we were doing was wrong - I mean he was married and everybody relied on him and they were very strict - I know that - a lot stricter about family than people here. And there was me: getting married in five days time; my white lace dress hanging in tissue paper in the wardrobe; a reception for sixty and a honeymoon in Greece all booked. We'd talked about nothing else for months.

It'll be the happiest day of your life, people said... the happiest day...

At that moment down on the pier, I couldn't be bothered with it. My cheeks were blazing hot. What was I worrying about? It wasn't as though we were doing anything illegal, immoral. We were just two school friends having a chat...

"Caroline," he said.

We were standing by the metal rail at the end of the pier. The wind was slamming his black hair across his face. I couldn't speak because he had said my name and the way he pronounced it made it so intimate. But I still wanted to tell him.

"I've missed you so much," he said.

I couldn't look at him although I knew he was gazing at me.

"Why did you let your parents walk over you, then?"

The hurt of it boiled in my chest and my heart was banging. The year we were eighteen he did go to India for a holiday. He'd promised to tell me all about it. I'd really envied him. And then when he'd returned, he'd been quieter, different. That was when I began to be frightened of all those white temples and sacred cows and the sarees and the wailing music and the gods. I stopped finding them magic.

Raj was my first lover. We used to sneak back to my house during free periods or games lessons when we were in the sixth form. My Mum and Dad would be out at work, but we were still scared stiff somebody would find out. It was like a craziness. If we couldn't see each other we'd be going mad. And then one Wednesday afternoon, after he'd made my lips swollen with kissing and between my legs was sore, he suddenly said: Caroline, I won't be able to see you again.

What do you mean? I felt I'd received a hard slap across my face. Nothing like that had ever happened to me before.

His parents were having a bride sent from India.

But you're your own person, you don't have to do what they say...

He couldn't answer that. He just seemed to retreat into himself and wouldn't respond.

When's she arriving, then?

Next month.

That was the summer we left school.

I mustn't ever come here again.

And he didn't and we finished school that July and that was the end of it. Only it wasn't because I couldn't forget him. I went to see that film, 'Gandhi', and it made me cry. By then I was with Warren who found it boring. Many a time I hesitated by their shops, longing to go in, but I wouldn't.

I didn't expect him to answer my question and the silence was just filled up with the crashing of water and the foghorn mooing. Then he said:

"I didn't have any option."

"No?"

"No - what could I have done at eighteen? I ask you, Caroline? You don't know what it's like for us..."

'Us' he said, as though he was different - another sort of human being.

"Well, never mind - it's a long time ago - it was just that I've been waiting to ask you..."

"Oh, my God, I've regretted it, don't think I haven't."

We looked at each other then and I wanted to cry because of the six years that had gone by and the discovery that the thing between us was still there. It was like he'd put a stamp on me that wouldn't fade away or rub out: I was his and I think I hated him for it.

There are all those love songs where people wail about wanting to be set free, well it was like that. I understood them. I'd been with quite a few men during the time since but none of them was like him: there was something missing - no excitement, no thrill, no mystery, no suffering sweetness. Raj only had to look at me and the live wire threaded between us.

I don't know how long we stood at the rail just gazing out to sea at the dark indistinct masses of ships on the skyline. You could set sail on those brown waves and travel all over the world to anywhere - they were fathomless - they could kill you or buoy you up. They might be poisoned with deadly chemicals from the B.P. works, but they were still beautiful - savage and beautiful.

"Why did I have to meet you today?" I said. I was trembling. He looked very dark on the pale winter afternoon, dark and foreign. Oh, I've always loved exotic things... I've wanted them to cancel me out.

Nobody would ever know this when they see me sitting at my VDU screen in the office of the senior partner. I'm just efficient, well-groomed, bright and bushy-tailed. I know all the answers... at least my boss thinks I do.

"It had to happen," he said.

"Look, I'm getting married next week and I don't want to be thinking about you." I was sure my mascara must be smudged all round my eyes but it didn't matter, none of it mattered beside the pain. I just wanted to be alone with him in a room and I wanted him to kiss me, touch me - if we could just tear off each other's clothes, eat each other up... The wanting was in his face too, in the way his eyes stared. But we didn't do anything; we stood a few feet apart and looked.

"All right," he said, "but you will be - there isn't any way out."

"Don't say it."

"You know it's true - that's how it is."

"Just leave me, Raj," I said, "I'd like to think of you down here..."

"Caroline."

"No... I'll walk back... it's fine."

He could see I meant it. This was worse than that afternoon years ago when we were kids. The street lamps had come on and everything was caught in an eerie twilight. How I wanted him to hold me and I know he felt the same.

"I wish I'd been someone else," he said.

"Don't say that."

We hesitated a long time and then he turned away and went back to his car. I stood watching the waves that were almost black now and the force of the water vibrated the planking. I could never be like I'd been at sixteen. He'd ruined me for anything else with all those stolen afternoons. And I was getting married in five days time to Warren, who's kind and blundering and totally without imagination; and the front room at home was piled up with wedding presents - toasters, sheets, towels, a duvet, vases, clocks, a microwave. My Mum and Dad were giving us a washing-machine... all sorts of things that made a fortress.

I heard his car start up and drive off and then I began walking back into town to get my bus.

Three months have passed since then. The wedding was a great success - or so everyone said. They say I look radiant in the photos. My Mum has had the pictures mounted in a special wedding book that chimes 'Here Comes the Bride' when you turn the pages. Some of the guests have camcorders so now we've got a video of everything, which my Mum shows endlessly.

I know now what Raj must have felt like when they were placing garlands round his neck and chanting. You go on with these things because it's what people expect. This unbounded ferocious emotion hasn't got anything to do with marriage and families, washing-machines and mortgages.

It's a funny afternoon. The sky's lemon-coloured. I can see it from the window. I'm at work. My boss is out. Bright green letters jerk across the screen. The phone rings.

"Dawson & Proctor - Mr Dawson's secretary, can I help you?" I twitter.

"Caroline."

My heart's bounding and I'm out of breath like I've been running in a marathon.

"Yes," I say.

Neighbours

I keep what you might call an immaculate house - oh, yes I do. I'm very particular about personal cleanliness as well. I mean, when I'm getting Bri's tea ready, I always wear an overall but even then I have to shower and wash my hair after if I'm going to work or out. It doesn't do to smell of bacon and eggs or fish and chips, does it?

We're throwing one of our parties tonight. We have a lot of friends - I generally invite all the ones in from our cul de sac. Some of them are a bit stodgy - like Steff and Carl. She's nice, got a lovely smile and a raggedy perm, but they're so quiet. Still, it doesn't do to have too many extraverts leaping about. I've made it quite clear that I don't want anything marking. Usually I make the guys and dolls take their shoes off at the door because our hall carpet's light beige and the through-lounge's cream shagpile. Bri thinks it's too unfriendly to do that at parties, so I'm leaving it this time, though I shall be watching with my eagle eye - I don't miss much.

The cars have started arriving. You can always tell who's going to be first. Bri lets them in. I'm in the bedroom frantically squeezing into this flame-coloured number with the plunging front. My underwired bra gives me a nice uplift.

Steff and Carl are walking through the front door as I'm coming downstairs.

"Hi, Carole," Carl says, "nice dress."

"Thank you, kind sir," I beam.

Bri's just put on a compact disc of some smoochy music. I think it's far too early for anything like that. Anyway I know a lot of them will want Heavy Metal or Rap and there'll be some tussles over it.

Well, the serious drinking's started. They're in the kitchen pouring wine and tearing into the six-packs of lager and knocking back the Newki brown. I never like it when they swig from bottles and cans because it can end up on your floor, but that seems to be the way of things. I'm wondering if they've brought anything in on their feet. There are all these types who walk their dogs round here and of course they leave their calling cards outside my front door. I know one guy who got so mad, he bought an air gun and tried to shoot at this poodle... well, he missed and shot himself in the foot.

It's while I'm circulating with bowls of salted peanuts and nibbles that I notice Steve. I'm holding this glass of nibbles out to him and he's not taking any notice. He's staring at Steff. Steve is part of a couple. His partner, Lindsey, is in the kitchen because I've just seen her. She's talking about diets and going to 'Weight Watchers' with a couple of other girls. Now Steve is very quiet and Lindsey is a big blonde who talks a lot and laughs. She's always the heart and soul of the party - she has this perfect skin and teeth and big blue eyes and lots of blond curls. You never seem to notice Steve because of Lindsey; it's Lindsey who's going to step-aerobics and drama and photography - Steve drifts along in her wake.

I kind of see him for the first time because he's so busy gazing at Steff. He's scrawny, dark and intense.

Steff's wearing this little black dress with shoe-string straps, red shoes and red dangly earrings. She's staring at him too. It makes me feel I've missed something.

"Here, Steve," I say, smelling his 'Aspen', "get some nibbles."

I know I'm interrupting a private matter.

"Oh, thanks, Carole," he says, and he's like somebody in a trance. His eyes are glassy.

I squeeze in and out amongst the groups. If they walk anything into my carpet, I'll go mad.

A few are smooching. Bri's in a corner with his golf cronies. In the kitchen Lindsey's rocking on a high stool at the breakfast bar and stuffing sausages and chunks of cheese into her mouth and gulping down her wine.

"Cheers, Carole," she says, "come and join us!"

"Oh," I say, "I'm just keeping an eye on things - have to play the hostess."

"Let Bri do his whack for a change!"

I'm never sure about Lindsey. You kind of think she's on your side but then the next thing, she's sucking up to the men - she's very tricky.

I go back into the lounge. I want to see what's happening. They're all jammed together with plates in their hands, chomping up the food and talking. It's the usual stuff about prices and schools and houses and mortgages and jobs and redundancies and golf and football. I suddenly think: Hell, I've heard this lot before. I wish they'd all go home so's I can get the mess cleaned up.

Steve's standing next to my neighbours.

"Well, you never know, I mean nobody's sure of their jobs these days, are they?"

"No," Steve's saying. But I notice that although he's pretending to be listening to our neighbour, he isn't really; he can still see Steff across the room. She's nodding her head and talking to somebody, but she's peeking at Steve every now and then.

Steve and Lindsey haven't got any kids. Carl and Steff have two little boys, three and four. She's always taking them to the leisure centre and to the park to feed the ducks. Carl works in the Community Charge office. They're very happy from what you can see - one of these nice quiet couples. Her house is spotless and her kids never look scruffy; she wears minis and little tops and you'd think she was about fourteen.

Darran from next door suddenly turns to me, "Come on, Carole, let's have a smooch." So we start dancing a bit by the french windows.

"We're saving up for a conservatory," I tell Darran. "I want a patio and one of them real nice what-do-you-call-its?"

"A gazebo," he says.

"Yes, that's right - I've always fancied one like you see in the ads - white paint and glass - and I'll have a sun-lounger in there."

I'm facing into the room and, over Darran's shoulder, I see Steve making his way across to Steff. Her eyes are real wide open and staring - then I can't see her face anymore because Steve's standing in front of her.

The next thing, I see both of them leaving the lounge. I have to know where they're going.

"Darran, my feet are killing me, I'll have to stop."

He shrugs. I slide round people and reach the hall, just in time to see both Steff and Steve going into the bathroom at the top of the stairs. I can't believe it. It makes me gasp and takes my breath away. I have to go to our bedroom for my inhaler and have a few puffs, then I feel better. I mean, it's disgraceful. What can they be doing in there? I don't want something like this happening in my house - it's not right, is it? In my bathroom. Bri's plumbed in the shower and the rose pink washstand and done the rose-bud tiles right up to the ceiling and the low pedestal siphonic loo. It's a lovely bathroom, I'll say it myself.

He'll be running his hands down that little black dress, maybe undoing the zip and she'll be naked at the top and wearing suspenders and a waist slip and maybe no pants and he'll press her against the washbasin and try to get in that way, but he won't be able to because he's too big and she's too small. They're lying on the fluffy pink rug next to the bath. She's under him...

I keep peeping through the bedroom door. Somebody's knocking to get into the bathroom. It's our neighbour from two doors up. She waits and then goes back downstairs. Two or three more try the door, then leave off and go back down.

How dare they do this in my house? I can't believe it. What will everybody think?

Funny how I never noticed anything about Steve before - he's always been this thin dark guy who doesn't stand out in a crowd - and now he's changed into something else. It's his eyes. They look like he's seen things other people haven't - he's sad and hot and terrible all at once. I don't believe what's happening. If I was Lindsey or Carl, I'd be breaking that door down, I'd be taking a knife to them - yes, I would. I couldn't bear to think of what they're doing. What if Bri does things like this as well? How would I know? Perhaps everybody's got these other lives going on all the time. I find goosepimples pricking up on my arms. Maybe Bri's not neat and gingerish, a nice considerate guy - but a six foot five Viking in black leathers. Perhaps nothing's what it seems at all. I have to have another couple of puffs on my inhaler.

The door's opening. Through the chinks in the hinges, I can see them coming out, first him, then her. They're going downstairs, cool as you like. What a neck they've got!

I leave it a couple of minutes and then I follow them down.

She's back in the lounge with a group of other girls - he's in the kitchen fetching himself a lager. I can see Lindsey's still holding forth and everybody's doubling up with laughter. Nobody's noticed anything. He wanders back into the lounge. I can't help staring at his back - his Levis fit him dead snug and his black polo shirt's tucked in. His hair's shaved very close to his skull at the back and he's got a firm, wide neck - very smooth and quiet he is. It frightens me all of a sudden to think about him. I mean he's not what you'd think at all. And nobody knows any of this - I can see they don't. A lot are totally bombed out, or they're telling one another things and nobody's noticed these two.

Then Carl comes over with Steff.

"Carole, thanks for a lovely party, we'll have to be off... baby-sitters." It's Carl who talks. Steff just stands beside him, smiling and nodding. Her make-up is perfect. You'd have no idea... I can't stop looking at her. Does he really know what's going on and he's pretending not to? Impossible. He'd kill Steve if he had any idea of what he's done with Steff. Did I see Steve and Steff go into the bathroom or am I going dotty? I know I did...

When they've nearly all lurched off home, I find Lindsey's still in the kitchen with a group round her. She's in the middle of a story and Steve's lolling against the breakfast bar, part of the audience.

Lindsey and Steve are the last to leave.

"It's been a brilliant party, Carole, love!" and Lindsey gives me a massive hug. She's all soft and warm and it's like sinking into 'Dunlopillow' and she smells of 'Obsession' mixed with cheese and onion crisps and booze.

"Bye, Carole," Steve says. His eyes are a real dark blue and he has pink cheeks and the black hairs are curling out of the neck of his polo shirt. I try to stop staring at him.

Bri comes up, when we've finally shut the front door.

"Do you want us to get started on the kitchen first... or shall we do the lounge?" He knows my routine - I can't sleep until everything's straight.

"No, love, leave it..." He looks surprised. I take his hand and lead him upstairs. When we reach the bathroom door, I push it open and draw him in. I don't put on the light but I can see the faint glimmering of the mirror and I can smell 'Aspen' and something else. Then I'm pushing my tongue into his mouth and hands are pressing me against the washbasin.

IRON Press was formed in Spring 1973, initially to publish the magazine IRON which more than two decades, and more than 1,500 writers on, survives as one of the country's most active alternative mags – a fervent purveyor of new poetry, fiction and graphics. £12.00 gets you a subscription. Try our intriguing book list too, titles which can rarely be found on the shelves of mega-stores. Fortified by a belief in good writing, as against literary competitions or marketing trivia, IRON remains defiantly a small press. Our address is at the front of this book